Also by Alan Franks

Fiction:

Boychester's Bugle

Plays:

The Changing

The County Man

Our Boys

A Wing and a Prayer

The Mother Tongue

Me and Madonna

The Edge of the Land

Previous Convictions

Augusta

Song albums:

Will

Ladders of Daylight

The Arms of the Enemy

Bird in Flames

Journalism: Real Life With Small Children Underfoot

Poetry: Collection of poems and song lyrics by published by Markings Magazine

GOING OVER

Muswell Press Ltd
www.muswell-press.co.uk

Going Over by Alan Franks
Text Copyright Alan Franks 2009

First Published in Great Britain November 2009
ISBN 978-0-9547959-7-9

A CIP record of this book is available from The British Library.

Book design by THIS IS Studio / www.thisisstudio.com
Cover Photo: Collections/James Paul
Printed and bound by JF Print Ltd, Sparkford, Somerset

Muswell Press Ltd
www.muswell-press.co.uk

For Ruth

Going Over

Last year, having finally agreed to see my father, I decided to make a detour first. I suppose there were two ideas behind it. If the trip was a disaster, I could at least tell myself that I had done something else as well. Also, it would buy some time between the easy bit of setting off and the difficult bit of arriving. But how much time, and how much space? Too little and it would just be an extension of the journey. Too much and it would become the object itself. So eventually I settled on a distance of about 80 miles and a time of four or five days, bearing in mind that I was walking. I bet he never had such difficulties with his own calculations, the old sod.

I would pick up the path at the Lion Inn, high up and entirely alone on the North Yorkshire Moors at Blakey. I had already done the eastern section of the coast-to-coast route as a boy of 12, coming westwards from Robin Hood's Bay via Grosmont and Glaisdale. In fact I had done it with my father in the hot summer that started up so soon after the unmentionable events of Easter, the two of us walking in silence along the flat, empty tops. I had no wish to revisit that occasion as well. This present trip was quite enough to be going on with.

If I walked west from Blakey, as far as Shap, I would have done two thirds of the coast-to-coast and could pick up the final section, across the Lake District to St. Bees Head, on a later occasion. This is how I have always done the long distance routes, collecting them in parts over a series of years: two summers for the Pembrokeshire Coast, three for Offa's Dyke, and so on.

The routes made their way into my life like good novels, and then helped to define my memories of the periods that surrounded them. It is ironic that if it had not been for my father I would probably not have spent so many long days of my own adult life on the upland paths of England, stalking the deep satisfaction of tiredness and inns. For his part he used to thank J.B. Priestley who, in his book *An English Journey*, wrote about the meditative properties of walking, the "skull cinema" that comes into play when you put one foot in front of the other and let the miles pass beneath them.

It's true. When I live for days on my striding feet a kind of hypnosis occurs. The result is an intense awareness of the place, but a removal from the moment. There is a shifting of time. Past events stand up like boulders in the foreground, and present concerns recede to a point on the rear horizon.

Then there was the other old man, Alfred Wainwright. He was the one who pioneered a walking route from one side of the country to the other, all along public rights of way, and was generally reckoned to be a Great Englishman. I took a conscious decision to do my walk without the benefit of his guide book. In keeping my independence from him I was also asserting my freedom from paternal influence. Childish, I'm sure.

Years ago I met Wainwright a few times, always through my father, and heard him complain about the number of people crowding the hills. I wanted to tell him that many of these people went on account of his recommendations but, as so often, I didn't quite dare. Then he turned his complaints towards bus fare prices, the performance of Blackburn Rovers and the decline of ledger calligraphy in town hall finance departments. "You should be able to frame each page," he said, "and hang it on your wall." I seem to remember my father trying to humour him, but this was rather like one undertaker trying to jolly another along. I wondered if they were really only happy in the act of complaining. Some time later, on the radio, I heard Wainwright say he'd drawn the hills so that he would be able to recall them when he could no longer walk on them, but now that he could no longer walk he'd lost the sight to see what he had drawn.

Not long after that he died. Everyone said what a fine man he was and seemed frightened of saying a word against him, even when it couldn't get back to him. I never let on about hearing him say, not long before the unmentionable events, how he preferred the company of the hills to the women he'd married; or about my father grunting in agreement; or about me hoping that I wasn't going to turn out like that. I would rather have suffered the consequences of open blasphemy than tell those men that I was going to do a thing a different way from them.

But I'm digressing. I can feel the detours trying to push my story from its course at every turn. If they were the detours on a walking route I could handle them. I could give them their head and be sure, from my years of experience, that I could map-read my way back onto the correct path. But they are not. They are unexpected, unmarked. I do not know where they will go, nor whether they will start to assert themselves as the proper destination, nor even whether they will offer a way back onto the original route. They are as forbidding as they are tempting. I fear and regret them, even though I know my journey would be duller without them. The more I proceed with it, the more I feel that I must lose my way in order to find it. That at least is not a completely new sensation.

I booked a room at The Lion. I did this by phone a week in advance. I have heard too many stories of people turning up there, finding it full, and having to try their luck with the landladies of Castleton. I believe Wainwright writes that "there is a ruin across the road where a miserable night could be spent." But I am nearly fifty, and solvent, and my days of sleeping like an animal are behind me, I think.

Nowadays, when I am away, I find myself looking at the number of stars next to the hotels in the guidebooks. I give guest houses a miss. No more shiny sausages in the front rooms of widows' houses. No more framed photos of graduating children. No more baths that run tepid after four inches. I go to places where the little basket of shampoo bottles gets replenished every day. I take them with me when I leave, but I have no interest in the shower caps. I hate the Corby trouser presses, and once immobilised one by yanking its metal arms out to the side. I can't really say why I did this. It was a sort of indulgence, a very delayed treat for a child that had never managed to misbehave – not properly anyway. I did it because I could – the same reason that gross Americans overeat. I probably did about £30 pounds worth of damage, more than I have knowingly done in the rest of my life. It felt great. I have also had two breakfasts, pretending to be two different people – a swarthy one who gets stuck in at 7.00, and then a clean-shaven one who saunters in at 10.00, just before they whip the stuff away. Not that I'd be able to get away with this kind of thing at The Lion , which only takes a handful of guests.

I took the Newcastle train from Kings Cross, then changed at Darlington for Middlesborough and the little line east to Whitby via Commondale and Egton Bridge. I got out at Danby and took a local taxi up to Blakey and The Lion. I had a bright new Karrimor rucksack, and could see that the driver had me down as a Southern Wanker. I was impressed by the sheer volume of contempt he managed to pack into the words "Walking then, are you."

The rucksack, I admit, was a mistake. Beth bought it for me in a sale at the YHA shop. As we had only been living together for six months, I couldn't bring myself to tell her it was horrible - a purple and yellow clash of alarming violence. In those days we were circling our way round each other here in the West Hampstead flat, holding on to the early politeness, terrified of the angers that intimacy was bringing as its inevitable freight.

Now, nearly two years into our unspoken contract, I would tell her how hideous I thought it was. But then now she wouldn't buy that sort of thing. Or if she did, I would make sure it got stolen, as I eventually did with this one. I know she was only wanting to express her support for this passion of mine. But that was where the problem lay. She thinks it's profoundly odd of me to go walking when the country is criss-crossed by perfectly adequate roads and railways, and so any expression of support was bound to misfire. Still, I thanked her for it at the time, in the way I had been brought up to thank people.

I should also thank her for making me write this. She knows even less than I do what the contents will be. What she does know is that for the past year and a half, since I came back from the walk and the visit, there has been something preoccupying me, syphoning my attention away from people and things without warning. It is strange that this should have coincided with the period when she and I have grown so close, so virtually married. Many times, in bed, in the bath, on the heath, I have nearly talked about it, nearly told her everything, and then pulled back at the last minute. And every time this has happened, the resulting silence has been very deep, as deep as a lake, like the silence in which I walked with my father from Robin Hood's Bay to The Lion Inn when I was twelve and he was the age I am now.

Then, a few months ago, Beth suggested I should write it down. We had just made love. She was lying on her side, with her head on my chest, and I had gone distant again. "If you write it down," she said, "then it's out of you. You've taken its power away." This is the kind of thing she often says when she has just come back from her group. It might sound as if I am threatened into cynicism by that sort of remark, but I am not. Anything that makes me savour the divergence between my father and me, rather than dread the convergence, is welcome. Besides, what she says is true.

I even like the other women in the group, although I can understand why Beth is wary of me establishing too much direct communication with them. She thinks I fancy Jo, the thin one who used to be a model, and she is absolutely right, although obviously I would never do anything about it. It would be very hard for men not to fancy Jo.

"You'll find your feelings change when you write it down," Beth said. Of course I immediately thought this was her means of getting me to tell her what was on my mind (out of the question), but I was wrong. The following day I began scribbling down some rough notes. I started with The Lion Inn because that was the linking point between the walk as a boy with my father and the one without him as a man. It was the end of the first and the beginning of the second. It seemed to offer me the promise of a structure as I wrote. This structure feels at times circular, at times linear. I say I have to thank Beth for the suggestion, but I find myself doubting whether it will be a matter for gratitude. It keeps taking me into exposed places for which I have no maps. I don't think I will be showing any of this to her. I believe that I love her. I am less sure that she could she love me back if she found out what I am about to write; if she were to discover the truth of my genetic inheritance.

I nearly find myself writing that I made the journey because my father was in his late eighties and would not go on for ever. But only the first half of that statement seemed true. The reason I went is that Maud wrote to me. She had been his housekeeper for a while, before becoming something more. She certainly moved in with him and possibly married him to make it all look proper. If not, then they were just another man and woman living together, as Beth and I are. I was glad of Maud's presence as it stood conveniently between him and me. She was nearly twenty years younger than him, and clearly digging in for a substantial Third Age of her own.

Her letter was brief and functional, saying what a good idea all round it would be if the "old boy" and I could see each other. She said she wrote with his blessing, and although I did not disbelieve her I had a notion that she had her own reasons for wanting the meeting. I had very indistinct memories of her, despite being aware of her presence in the village from my earliest days. She came from a family full of women who lived above the shops. They took turns to work in the general store and no-one could remember which was which. They supplemented their income with service of various sorts in the large outlying houses. They had all been evacuated from the little village of Mardale when the water board flooded their valley in 1939. Yet Maud's name conjured nothing in my mind beyond an apron and a slightly austere head of hair. When I then spoke to her on the phone to fix the date of my visit, she sounded friendly enough, if a little cautious. It was strange to think of her as a resident of that old stone house at the end of the straggling little town, just as I had once been.

The drive from Danby to the Lion Inn took nearly half an hour. There was something perverse and glorious about taking a taxi up into the middle of nowhere on a summer evening. Up and up we went, with Danby clinging to us like a brand name. Danby Low Moor behind us, Danby High Moor ahead, Danby Rigg to the left, Danby Beck to the right, Danby Dale beneath the wheels, Danby Cars on top of the roof. When the inn came into view I heard myself say "That's it" helpfully, just as I might if I have spotted the right turning in north London.

"That's lucky," he replied without a smile as I got out and paid him. I gave him an insincerely large tip and, through my VAT habit, asked for a receipt. He tore one from his pad and gave it to me blank. His face was saying "I know what you lot get up to" as he swung round in the car park and drove off.

As soon as I was shown to my room above the bar I realised it was the same one that my father and I had stayed in thirty seven years before. In those days the place did not regularly take overnighters, and my father must have cajoled one of the staff into letting us stay. As I unpacked my sponge bag, I could vaguely remember him remonstrating with someone about charging for "the boy." His anger was so obviously bigger than everyone else's, and so obviously more imminent that no-one ever bothered to question him. It would be like questioning a front of heavy weather. The front may not be right, but it was coming. The absence of challenges reinforced his sense of infallibility. If he was wrong, he argued, then people would tell him so, just as he would tell them. And if they weren't man enough to speak their mind, then their opinions weren't worth having anyway. And on it went: north better than south; League better than Union; old better than new; and women running the town halls over his dead body. Of course, this did not explain what had happened between him and my mother, but it helped a little.

I had dinner in the bar of the Lion, with the Ordnance Survey map, Number 93, flapping and falling off the edge of the table. The next day's places along the route set up a striding rhythm in my head. I cast my eyes across from east to west, as far as the edge of the Cleveland Hills and the beginning of the Vale of Mowbray. After that there would be a whole sheet of OS map, Number 92 before I cleared the Pennines, crossed the Westmorland Plateau and had to contemplate the approach of the old stone house and its disdainful coldness in the height of this tremendous summer.

I could have come at it the other way, from St. Bees Head on the west coast. That would have entailed a straightforward crossing of the Lake District, reliably glorious but full of people. Alfred Wainwright of course was a west-to-east man. I remember my father and him falling into a heated disagreement about the best direction. That must have been 20 years ago, the last time I had seen my father, just before I was 30 and when they were already white-haired old boys with opinions cast in long-vanished foundries. East to west is the way, said my father, because you keep the best until last. No, said Wainwright; always best to keep the weather at your back. My father feigned deafness and they went, literally, their own ways. Now I was going in my father's direction, and this filled me with ambivalent feelings.

After dinner I settled the bill for the night, knowing I would be up at 5.00 the next morning and gone before the place was stirring. I was in bed by ten. I phoned home and left a message on the machine for Beth, who was at her group. Then I returned to the map and went on all manner of flights across the 1:50,000 landscape, flitting from rigg to rigg, and clearing whole river systems at a hop. High above Spaunton Moor, with the abbey crouching no bigger than a beetle at the foot of it, I could feel myself dropping towards sleep. I was dimly aware of someone singing, but could not be sure whether the sound was coming up from the bar or across all the years since I was last here. It was *"She Moves Through The Fair"* and it was being sung by a high-voiced man or a low-voiced woman. I could hear some of the lines, about the swan in the evening moving over the lake, and about it not being long, love, till our wedding day. I strained for more, but without success. Whatever stood between it and me became more unbridgeable by sound. If the obstacle was the floor of the room, it grew thicker carpet; if it was the years, they stretched out like a chain of passed valleys.

"The boy should learn to look after himself," says my father.

"For pity's sake," says my mother. "He's just twelve years old."

"That's what I mean, woman. That's what I'm saying. It's time he got wise. Time he got tough."

"And do you think he'll be interested in dragging himself along those moors in your wake, with you not slowing for him and quite happy to sleep like an animal?"

"Interested doesn't come into it," says my father. "It's what he'll be doing."

They think I can't hear them from where I am. But I'm little and quiet, and I know where to go. I know the places that let the sound of their voices in. There are more of the hearing places when their voices are raised. I can slide up and down the three storeys of our narrow house and not be noticed by them. They are too busy arguing to think about me. Sometimes I dislike her almost as much as I dislike him. I don't want to, but I do. It's good when it's just her and me. She's soft then. They must dislike me too. I must have put them off the idea of having any more children. I'm quite looking forward to being sent away to St. Bees. There will probably be other boys there like me. Other ones who have done something wrong but haven't been told what it is.

"You should ask me about it," says my mother.

"Ask be damned," he replies. He sounds very angry. "If I say he goes there, he goes." I don't know if he is talking about the walk over the moors, or going to school at St. Bees. It could be either. "Who is it earns the money in this house?"

"It's only you because you won't have me working."

"That's too right I won't. I won't have any wife of mine working."

"It's no favour you're doing me, Albert."

"Who's talking of favours?"

"Well for love then."

The word makes him even angrier and through the door I can hear him pacing the flags. The metal bits on the back of his heels come down hard and loud.

"Love," he says. "What kind of soppy talk is that?"

"It isn't soppy, Albert."

"Besides, who d'you think would have you in your condition?"

"What condition is that?"

"And you can't even see it."

When I woke up it was a quarter to five. I barely had to stir and the Lion started to creak. At once a dog chain clinked in the yard. Through the south-facing window I was aware of a fantastic dawn coming uninterrupted from the east. I got out of bed to dress and the creaking of the floor sounded like machinery in all that quiet. I padded downstairs in my socks, carrying my boots and rucksack. The place smelled of stale smoke caught in carpets, and a big hollow clock was ticking. I let myself out and saw the sun approaching in triumph like the sail of a land-boat. It was standing low in the sky and the shadows of the outhouses were as big as football pitches.

I set off to the right and was very soon on the down gradient of a fine broad track. Instead of progressing like a normal path, with bumps and improvisations, it went along in smooth and gentle curves, negotiating with the land for the benefit of the traveller. This was the trackbed of the old mineral line, an amazing piece of Victorian engineering that once carried the Rosedale ironstone over the moors to join the Middlesborough-Whitby line at Battersby Junction. I looked at the map and saw that the track contoured its way around these high shoulders at about 1300 feet.

Up here, for a short stretch of the way, you are doing four walks for the price of one: the mineral track, the Lyke Wake, the Cleveland Way and the Coast-to-Coast. That is the habit of open country these days. Old drove tracks and corpse roads become the components of a managed way which is then christened and marketed as a National Trail.

The sun reared up at my back, my stride lengthened, and I was clattering down the track at four, maybe five miles an hour. When I'm going this well, I can't imagine ever tiring or wanting to stop. By the time I crossed the road near Urra, two hours on from the Lion, I had still not seen another walker. Then the hills got up and started marching off to the west in a straight line: Hasty Bank, Busby Moor, Carlton Bank. They fell sharply away on the north side like a row of cliffs looking out to sea. Except that the sea here was a flat land of big fields and small settlements, with the tangled stacks of Middlesborough standing right at the other side of the view in a haze of their own making. Over Live Moor, down into Scugdale, across Coalmire and Scarth Nick. Then the hills called a halt, and beyond the main road at Ingleby there was nothing but the uneventful plain and the invisible Pennines beyond. The tarmac arrived and the names became tame: Oaktree Hill, Crowfoot Lane, West Farm. I should have stopped for lunch in the inn at Ingleby, but had lost track of the time. The heat baked the plain and buckled the air above it. The miles went mesmerically on. As they did so I waited for the far air to harden into the great barrier of hills which I knew to be there. I waited for it like a sailor waits for the next promise of landfall. I waited and waited, but still the wall did not appear.

"You heard," says my father. "I'll not spell it out again."

"You're too hard on him, Albert," says my mother.

"You don't know the meaning of hard. You don't know the meaning of nothing. Look at you."

She inspects herself and looks back at him. Her whole expression is wounded, like a bruise. They are standing on the middle landing, and I can see them from above. He goes on: "Who'd have you? You smell like a distillery every night of the week. And every morning you stink like there's a dead animal rotting in your gut. I can't take you to a function for fear of what they'll think. You've taken to shaking in the mornings."

"If I have, Albert, it's nothing but my nerves. I'll be better, I swear I will."

"You're only ever better when you take more of your poison. And then you're gone again, and around it all goes. You're known for it now. You're a known alcoholic."

"What a ridiculous word, Albert."

"I've tried to protect you all this time, but you've been on the stagger once too much. Where's the boy?"

"I don't know."

"And there's another thing."

"You know how he goes about."

"You're not fit. Once too much you've been. And all this while I'm trying to keep the lid on finance. Heather at the stores knows."

"Knows what?"

"Oh, the innocence of you. I've told her from now. No more bottles for you. It's finished."

"I can't think what you're on about, Albert."

"It's lies and all now, is it. I'll have no choice but to cut off the house-keeping and arrange for the boy myself. He's not here much longer. And no tick for you. No nothing. The disgrace of it."

When I looked ahead, I saw that the level of the horizon had gone up slightly. The wall of hills was showing itself at last. I was sharply reminded of my present situation by an angry voice telling me to stop where I was. My hand was just about to lift a loop of wire joining two fence poles in a rough gate arrangement.

"There's stock in there," said the voice, closer to me now. "You can't go through I'm afraid."

The farmer was about seventy, with an old quilted waistcoat even in this heat, and white woolly hair growing out from under his cap. He looked at me and my kit in much the same way as the taxi driver had done.

"It's a field," he said, with the plain tone of a primary school teacher.

These days I can go either way on such occasions. It all depends. When I was young I used to be absurdly deferential to people like this, and would gladly have made a detour into the next county so as not to upset him. But now I am more likely to stand toe to toe with them, rattling off the clauses of a by-law which may or may not exist. Twenty years of being an architect are probably responsible. I discovered that when builders told me a particular thing could not be done they sometimes based their arguments on non-existent regulations. It is all a matter of getting off to an assertive start. These battles are won and lost in the opening seconds. I once told Beth about my wimpishness and she said it was all about my father - about how I vested authority figures with his image and then complied with them. Only later - said Beth - had I come to challenge his dominance and then overcome him in conflict. I did wonder whether this was rather hard on the older men whom I had yet to encounter, who were condemned to be treated by me as though they were my tyrannical father. She laughed and said something like "Well, that's just how it works," as if I was naif to be questioning such a known truth. So then I wheeled in the figure of Oedipus, guaranteed to raise the temperature at times like this, and said that since I had effectively slain Laius it must mean that the woman I was now with was Jocasta, my mother. Beth wasn't happy about this, particularly when I said "Do you think we ought to look at this?"

Then we had one of our rows - very infrequent, I'm glad to say - with each of us blaming the other's family for everything. I wondered whether we were all condemned to land in our parents' selves, and whether the interim years were just a futile dance of evasion. She said something about my paths only being as they were because of what had been there before, and about how they were not just a connection between places but between times as well.

"If you want to get through," said the farmer, "the best way is out round the back there, then down that track, where my finger is, and out into Crowfoot Lane where us farmers don't go straying with our stock where it doesn't belong."

"Thank you," I said, "but this path is perfectly adequate for me."

"It's not a path is what I'm trying to tell you."

"Oh, but I'm afraid it is," I replied.

"Does it look like a path to you?"

"Well, not now that it has a bath across it, but it's no hardship to walk round that."

"I've told you like I've told the rest, I'll have you for trespass. All the others have gone round Crowfoot."

"I don't think you understand," I said, by now really quite disliking myself. "This is a right of way and it's registered on the definitive map."

"I don't have one of those."

"No, but the North Riding Council does. And under the Town and Country Planning Act of 1989 landowners must post a statutory notification of twenty eight days when applying for a diversion order." I haven't checked since, but now that we are talking figures, I am sure this is about ninety five per cent bogus.

He looked at me again and presumably thought briefly about a swift, unnotified act of violence. Instead he took off his cap and scratched his head, just like country people used to do in British films. I think he had me down as a solicitor, weighed up his odds of success and found them uneconomical. He lifted the loop of twine from the poles and let me through. I thanked him and carried on. He must have feared that I was going to report him anyway (I didn't, of course), because he called after me in his most sociable voice: "You've a grand day for it."

I wondered what my father would have made of this little episode. If he had been involved, there would have been no confrontation in the first place. The farmer would have sniffed a superior rage and backed off. Rather as I had done these past twenty years and more.

When I got to Danby Wiske I went into the White Swan and sank a pint of lager in two goes. They didn't do accommodation but knew a family who did. Before I could stop him the barman had the phone on the counter and was speaking to someone called Jen. He hung up and said "Jen and Brian will have you. Left out of the pub, straight up the road, cottage with the green gate, you can't miss it."

I phoned Beth from the call box on the edge of the green. The barman had offered me the use of the pub phone, without even knowing that I wanted to make a call. I can't bear using a private phone in public places. Everyone says they won't take any notice of you, but they tune in as hard as they can. That's the whole idea. Just because they are looking the other way they think you will assume they aren't interested. You tighten up, you can't make jokes or do voices, the person at the other end thinks something is wrong, and you can't explain that there isn't.

I told Beth about my encounter with the farmer, and she made mock-frightened noises. At least I think they were mock-frightened. At that stage in our relationship I could never be quite sure, and I am still prone to occasional doubts now. I fear the topic of violence, knowing her history of abuse as a child. Or knowing that such a history exists. She acknowledges it, but never goes into details. And I never press her, not just for fear of causing her pain but for the more selfish reasons of not wanting to be the target of a re-awakened anger. I'm fairly sure that the other women in the group know all the details. In a way, that is what they are there for. Whenever any of them come round and I am in the flat, I have the sense that they and I are squaring up, wondering what each other knows and doesn't know about Beth.

I told her how far I had walked from the Lion Inn to Danby Wiske, and she made the admiring noise which she knew I wanted to hear.

"Jo's here having tea," she said.

"That's nice," I said, as flatly as I could. The information was desperately erotic. My blood began pumping and I blushed. It was the thought of Jo's long, faultless limbs draped over my furniture. And it was the knowledge that she had no current boyfriend and was not, as far as I could gather, gay.

"Send her my," I said, not knowing quite what to send her. "Send her my best wishes."

"You are a formal old Englishman, aren't you."

"Oh probably."

"Jo sends her love."

I could hear slight laughter away from the phone.

"And she says to look after that Inner Child of yours."

"Oh, yes," I said. "Him."

"No, seriously," said Beth.".

"Seriously," I agreed. It was no laughing matter. As far as I could tell, all the women in the group had Inner Children, although very few of them had Actual Ones. For example: "My Child demanded an ice cream today, so I bought her one." In fact the person who ate the ice cream would turn out to be the woman. The thing about the Inner Children was that as long as their needs were being met they didn't obtrude into adult life. At least, not so that it showed. However, if their needs were not being met, then out they would come like bad girls after bedtime and things could get quite ugly. I once got into trouble with Beth over the issue and I had only myself to blame. We had just had sex. She mentioned that her Inner Child was happy and I asked if that made me a paedophile. Definitely a mistake.

Beth says that everyone has got one, including me. My father too, although I can't help thinking that if he ever came across it in the darkness of himself he would have had it fostered out.

"I'll tell you what though," I said. "I've just given the Inner Man a pint, and he's as happy as anything."

"I do sometimes wonder," said Beth.

"Wonder what?"

"Everything."

I told her I loved her, which was true but difficult. She sounded surprised and asked me whether I would say such a thing if I hadn't taken a drink. I think the truth was that I only said it because there were so many miles between us, but I couldn't very well tell her that.

Brian and Jen turned out to be a young couple with more children than I could count. I arrived to find him buried under a pile of them on the living room floor, and her trying to pick them off the top like boulders in a landslip. She kept saying "bedtime," but they took it as a signal to riot. When she stepped up the instruction to "bedtime now," they responded with an extra edge of urgency in the fighting.

Then, for no reason that I could see, they broke up and dispersed as if they were globules of mercury. Brian got to his feet, dusted himself down and apologised. If he thought I looked uncomfortable, it was because my own father was in my mind at the time, and I was thinking how far removed from mine were these children's experiences of childhood. If I had jumped on my father at bedtime, he would probably have...but the hypothesis was too wild to continue.

When the children next appeared, they were in pyjamas and smelling of toothpaste. They said goodnight to me without sniggering, and went off to bed. I would have gone to the pub for some food, but Brian and Jen insisted that I join them for dinner. With the sun of the day now burning its way back out of my face and the weight of the miles all stacked up in my legs, I nearly fell asleep at the table. I was aware of my mother and father waiting somewhere below to snare me in their terrible embrace. But they didn't get me. Not that night. Maybe I went down so far that I slipped beneath them.

Brian had just been laid off by a coach builder near Catterick, and was now driving an estate agent's van, putting up For Sale signs in the villages between Osmotherley and Richmond. He and his wife were taking in overnight guests to make ends meet. He asked me how far I was going, and when I told him Shap he said: "Well, you should see it if you're patient."

I looked puzzled, but before he could explain what he meant, Jen chipped in. "On the other hand," she said, "if you don't get a move-on you may not see it at all." It sounded like some folk riddle which I had to solve before I could leave. "Thou see'st me best who comes the latest, Likewise thou who this day hastest."

"Show him the *Echo*, love," said Brian. She took the paper from the dresser and handed it to me. There was a photo of an arid landscape with a narrow thread of water in it. In the foreground was a man with a tropical shirt, pointing back at the view. I assumed he must be a local man doing relief work in Africa or standing at the source of an undiscovered river. Then I read the accompanying caption: "The lost village of Mardale, near Shap, reappears as the drought continues to lower the level of Haweswater." Even in the grainy photo I could see the dry stone walls making their way across the dark grass of the steep fields and then carrying on down the bare, bleached ground.

"You see what I mean," said Brian. "It's getting lower every day. They say the church spire'll show through soon, and then all the houses around it."

"Not if it starts raining, they won't," said Jen.

"It's not going to rain. Forecast says we're in for a long drought."

"Well then we'd best all get our anoraks out, for all they know."

Brian took another look at the photo and said "Sad though, isn't it, a place being drowned like that."

Sad it was. It happened in the years just before the war, and was done to slake the mighty thirst of Manchester. They dammed the bottom end of Haweswater, cleared the village at the top and let the headwaters edge the lake level slowly up the sides of the valley. Although it happened many years before I was born, I remember my father going on about it at every opportunity, as if it was a current transgression. Since his value system insisted that country was good and big city was bad, this was a fine illustration of urban greed in action. The industrial prerogative had literally stolen a valley from beneath its people's feet. And goodness, his memory was long. Mardale, he pointed out, had been a secluded hamlet since the days of the Holm family. I assumed he was going back a few generations here, but it turned out he was referring to the time of King Stephen.

When I first walked up there as a boy of seven or eight, I could not understand why my father was shaking his head and tutting at the water. It looked like a fine, full lake to me, sitting in its basin just as it was meant to. Perhaps not quite as magnificent as Wast Water, but certainly grander and more dramatic than Windermere or Ullswater. "Look at that," he would say. "That's vandalism for you." It was confusing. For a while I associated vandalism with water in valleys, rather than with damage on housing estates, and yet my father said there was no finer landscape known to man than the English Lake District. Years later he and Wainwright were having a good old beef about it, their snowy old heads nodding away at their own correctness. I wanted to say that the valley looked OK with all that water in it, and that anyway Manchester needed the supply for employment and hygiene. My argument struck me as humane and rational, and yet the words died in me like heretics.

I took another look at the photo in the *Echo*. The sides of the exposed lake bed seemed to have developed contour lines, tightly ranged where the sides were steep, and spread more spaciously on the gentler slopes. They were evidently the successive low water marks of the subsiding surface. Although I could never share my father's opinions about the place, there was an easy nostalgia to be had from imagining the community that had once lived among its small fields and close houses. I could remember the stream that ran down sharply from the top end. To judge from the picture, this current of water still ran along its old gouge, even beneath the created lake. I wondered whether my father had got Maud to drive him up from Shap so that he could stand above the lake edge and survey the scene with his cold and antedeluvian purity. And I wondered what Maud had felt as the dryness laid bare the floors of her childhood, inch by inch. Whatever those feelings were, I did not think my father would have been aware of them. Once again the view would have to fit itself in as best it could behind the pillar of his anger. It was ironic that without the flooding and its consequences all our lives would have been different. Mardale altered their courses like diverted streams. Even across all the rugged miles which still stood between that place and me, I could sense the tension and expectation in the lake's slow emptying. It was a veil slipping from a place of secrets. There was a fear and a thrill in its coming off.

The next day was just as hot. "It's holding up for you," said Jen at breakfast. Considering the length of the previous day's walk, my legs were not suffering too badly. Perhaps all those preparatory walks on the Heath, some with Beth but most without, had paid off. The day ahead divided itself neatly into two. There was the last flat slog across the vale to Richmond, and then up Swaledale as far as Reeth.

I was walking west out of Danby Wiske by 8.30. I took big, fast strides to free myself from the tarmac as quickly as I could, and to defy the mild aches in my calf muscles. Before noon I was in Richmond. The town hardly knew what to be that day. The market place was baking in the heat and the old alleyways by the castle ruins were crawling with tourists. The Norman keep was hoarding huge quantities of time and history, and there were soldiers everywhere - off-duty men from the garrison at Catterick. I walked along Riverside Road and then turned right into Cravengate, eating Jen's cheese and pickle sandwiches. The day's journey so far was too short to give me that sense of a major arrival which walkers sometimes experience when they find themselves in built-up streets after long miles of nothing. In no time at all I was out past the Temple Grounds and heading up the suburban incline of Westfields.

Late in the afternoon, by way of Applegarth, Marske and Marrick, I came to the dale's *de facto* capital, Reeth, up on its open hillside. There was the thrill of elevation in the ground once more. In the high glory of mature day the landscape shook off the darker influence of Arkengarthdale, which came in like a corpse from the north. On more dismal days that great mined-out trench would cast such a grey mood as to make the whole region seem the victim of a spent klondyke. If it was vandalism my father was after, he should have looked here. Knowing that spoil and greyness would be the colour of my next day's walk, I filled myself with the greens of the valley and the silver flicker of its river as a man fills himself with food before crossing a barren time.

As Beth told me later, I must have courted the stones and the greyness as I could easily have stayed with the dale and then headed right at Muker. But I stuck with the southern reach of Melbecks Moor, stone-plated and utterly lifeless. It was as if the hills' old garments had been turned inside out and all the softness buried beneath bare lining. Here and there the components of the smashed ground had been worked up into sheds and chimneys and then left to fall back down into the pool of their parts.

From the ruins of the smelt mill at Surrender Bridge I headed up Old Gang Beck to Hard Level Gill. Stones climbed on stones, or else stood frozen into tumbling formations, like torrents that had been punished with petrification. Although the lead-mining which created this ground was long gone, the land was set to bear the scars forever. The land was the scars. It was pocked and shafted, shallow and deep. The peaks as well as the sides and bottoms. The hushes on the slopes were still stark enough to show the force of the water that had ravaged out the vegetation and the soil in search of a vein.

A hundred and fifty years ago there were thousands of men up here. Even the Romans had mined the seams, and they were probably not the first. Most of the good veins were worked out by the end of the nineteenth century, and the ones that weren't were being undercut by the cheap imports from Spain. From Hard Level Gill I followed the path along towards Lownathwaite Mine and Crackpot Hall. If I had stumbled unknowingly into the landscape, I might have taken it for the work of a stonemason on a massive commission. In spite of the season, in spite of the weather, I passed no-one all morning, and had only my footsteps for company. There were no animals, no insects, and nothing for the birds, who wheeled away from the air above it. The footsteps sounded hollow and enclosed, like an anxious heart in a forbidden place.

"I've been passed over," says my father.

"Oh, I'm sorry to hear that, Albert," says my mother.

They have come across each other once again on the landing. And once again I am looking down at them from the floor above.

"Sorry is it? Is that all it is?"

"I don't see how I can be more, Albert. If you'd set your heart on it, then, as I say, I'm sorry."

"You make it sound like a toy in a shop, and a lad coveting it for his birthday."

"Well, perhaps it is a little like that. And I'd feel sorry for the lad and all."

"You've been drinking, haven't you."

"No."

"It's not a question, it's a statement."

"Then you've no need to be asking me."

My father is right. I saw her in the kitchen while he was out, her hands clasping a tumbler of something misty, and her face staring down into it as though there were important secrets at the bottom. She looked like she wanted to be on the other side of its surface, but couldn't work out how. So she drained it, and made a painful face, and filled it again from a bottle in a paper bag.

"Drinking you've been. Oh the stink's coming up from the floor of you."

"I tell you, I'm sorry you've been passed over, Albert, but there's nothing I can do about it."

"No, you've done all there is to do, so you're right on that count. Why would they put me up at the head of a department when I've a wife who'll disgrace us all at the first function?"

"I wouldn't have come and got in your way. I'd have shoved off."

"What kind of wife is that? Staying away when she's most needed."

"I've never got on with the other wives. You know that."

"They're decent women and they support their husbands."

"That's as may be."

She is unsteady on her feet and in her voice, but she is standing up to him. I wish she would do it without a drink as she would be so much better at it, but I suppose that without the feelings the drink gives her she just shrinks away. My father steps back from her as if he is taking a better look. Then he starts again.

"The condition of you. Do you think I don't know where you got it from this time?"

"Got what, Albert?"

"The Devil's truly made from liquid, isn't he. Stop him off and he goes by another course."

"I don't know what you mean."

"You'd go over the fells to Kirkby Stephen if the craving told you to. You'd fetch up with bleeding feet and think nothing of it."

They circle each other a little. She wants to end this conversation. I think she is more afraid of herself than of him. I think she is worried about what she might say or do.

"It takes you off," he says. His voice is raised. "It couldn't take you off more if it was another man. Adultery with the bottle is what it is."

My mother's head is hanging forward. Her shoulders give a little heave and I know this means the start of tears. But then she goes all tense and puts her fists up to her mouth like she is trying to force-feed herself with them. She does it to dam up the tears, because she knows they will annoy him even more. But she cannot control herself, and I hear the first sob. It makes the noise of an animal being forced from safety.

"And now the waterworks and all," he says. "Flood it all over would you. Anybody would think it was you and not me being passed over."

"It is," she says. "It is me."

"Oh and how's that pray?"

"You know perfectly well, Albert."

Suddenly she is sounding awfully composed and normal, just like other mothers when they are having words with their husbands. He too stiffens and pulls his shoulders back. She is coming to something. But then she stops again.

"What do I know perfectly well?" he says.

"Well, you know her name, I expect."

"Name? Whose name?"

"In the store."

He begins to stutter and splutter. Martin, my friend from Bowness, says his grandfather did this just before he died. He says it is called a seizure. I wonder what would happen if my father just suddenly couldn't get any more air into him and conked out on the landing. The possibilities make me unable to think straight. It would be terribly exciting. Very sad, of course, particularly with him being such an active man. But very exciting all the same. People would look at me differently.

Then he recovers as well. It turns out he was only sort of tut-tutting into the air, but making rather a meal of it. He has gone red. I can see the colour on his forehead, and I don't know if it is out of anger alone or embarrassment as well.

"You've gone red, Albert," she says, very no-nonsense. "Just so's you know."

"I'll give you gone red," he says.

Now they are both bridling in their shoulders. Suddenly I find myself trying to imagine what each of them was feeling nearly fourteen years ago when they were in bed together, getting me. The thought of them, bare and tangled into each other, making noises and movements. But I can't get anywhere near it. The arms that they must have embraced with; they are raising them, shaking the hands on the end of them.

"You were seen, Albert. Up back of Kendal. On the Burneside Road."

"Was I now? Well that's very interesting because I don't ever go that route."

"Then someone must have influenced you."

"What are you talking about?"

"It was the weekend you were away with old Wainwright on the lead mine ruins. Or said you were."

"What does that mean? Said I was?"

Now it is his turn to try and answer her with two more questions, just as she was doing a moment ago when he was on the attack. They use each other's techniques, as boxing partners do.

"Said you were," she repeats.

"Are you calling me a liar?"

"Something else as it happens."

"Because no-one calls me a liar."

"Is it Maud is it?"

He does not answer. Instead he just looks at her and, I suppose, hopes that his look will make her words vanish. I think this has always been the way between them. But her use of that word, Maud, has changed everything, and they both know it. Instead of vanishing, it stands there, big as a boulder. Four letters, a single syllable, but nothing can get past it. Now other smaller words come tumbling around it; little rock-words.

"It is Maud, isn't it?" she says. She hardly believes her own boldness. And because she doesn't believe it she seems unafraid of it, and carries on.

"Only, I couldn't quite remember if it was Maud, or one of the other sisters from the stores. The ones who came over from Mardale when the reservoir went in. Ah well, Albert, I must say, I have to admire the neck of you for playing away so near home, if you follow me. I'd say they'd be most impressed at the council, your pals."

"Yer," he says. Then again: "Yer. Yer." This time it really does sound like a speech impediment. Or an end of speaking itself. It is meant to be the start of his next sentence, but the sound is damming him up. He can't talk, like my mother sometimes can't talk. It is his turn for the dumbness, and he will have to do something else now. Things will never be the same between them again. "Yer. Yer." The words sound like pushes. Then he puts his hand out, a bit like a buffer, and does actually push her in the shoulder. Yer, push. Yer, push. One day something dreadful will happen. I wish I could have my excitement in different ways.

When I reached Keld I phoned Beth. She asked if I was all right, in the way she has of implying that there is something not all right. I answered "Of course I am," but there must have been some clue in my voice which made her not quite believe me. I expect I was resentful that she had sensed some anxiety in me. This was one of the things I used to find hardest in our dealings when she first moved in. She could gauge my state of mind so effortlessly that it made a nonsense of my attempts to convey an impression of composure, or balance, or happiness, or whatever it might be at the time. She would just send it back, in the way a teacher (which is of course what she is) might send back a sloppy essay. I soon realised that these fronts of mine may have been good enough for the office, the sandwich bars, the tube, but they no longer passed muster at home. I might have rebelled, or screamed, or even called the whole relationship off. I'm sure she could sense this as well. To my surprise I found myself settling into the difficult comforts of being known. If I hadn't trusted Beth, if it hadn't all coincided with our first, tremendous period of sexual acquaintance, it might all have been different.

"How far have you walked today?" she asked.

"About twenty miles."

"Piece of piss."

"From Miss Couch Potato."

"So you're missing me then?"

"I am actually, yes."

It was true, and I think she was taken aback by it. What she couldn't have guessed - not even Beth - was the reason. The only way I could have explained it was by making her present with me - not up here at this dale head but at the top of the narrow stone house, looking down at another woman in another time. To do all that was far beyond my range, and made impossible by sundry barriers.

I knew her next question would be to ask me why I was missing her. I may not read her as clearly as she reads me, but I do sometimes get her right.

"Why are you missing me?" she asked.

"Well actually Beth, it's because I love you."

"What brought this on then? Apart from absence." She sounded a little bashful.

"You wouldn't understand," I said, and started to laugh. "It's true. You wouldn't."

"You haven't been drinking, have you?"

"Drinking? You know I don't."

"That's why I was asking."

"Right. Well I haven't been."

"Is it nice up there?"

"Up here?"

"Yes. Wherever you are."

"Nice. Yes, it's nice. It's quite weird actually."

"How, weird?"

"Well,"

"Or wouldn't I understand?"

"It's weird because you don't quite know what it's going to do next."

"Like me."

"I don't know. How do you know you don't know what you're going to do next?"

"I don't."

"Weird actually means that, doesn't it. Things to come. As in Weird Sisters. You're the teacher."

"And you're the clever one."

"Who says?"

"You do."

She talked for a while about the group. I knew there were confidences she would never breach, but she was good at offering pieces of information that lay tantalisingly on the surface of other people's lives. These details washed over me. I was still on the high landing, looking down on my parents' heads and unable to tell anyone what was going on. There was no Beth. There was no anyone.

"Oh, and Jo's pregnant," said Beth.

"Jo?"

"Yes. Come on, you know Jo."

"Pregnant."

"But the thing is, she's gone very coy about who the father is."

"I see."

Ridiculously, I felt myself blushing, and glad this was only a telephone conversation. I keep waiting for the end of inappropriate guilt, but it doesn't arrive. Sometimes it makes me come out with the stupidest things, as I now did when I said: "It wasn't me, was it?"

The next day the land tipped over. This was the part of the crossing where I felt most forcefully the journey's lateral nature. Until now I had been walking against the grain of the country while the water courses passed me like oncoming traffic. Now I was up towards the watershed at Nine Standards Rigg, beyond Raven Seat and Coldbergh Edge. Nature needed no help from industry to lay a scene of desolation here. Even the main artery that goes over from Keld to Nateby is no more than a tarmac ribbon through wild moorland. After just a few days in the open I could sense the shift in the ground's arrangements. Instead of heading off into the Swale and being caught in the drainage system that carried everything to the North Sea, the indents of the becks, gills and tiny runnels started tending the other way, towards the tributaries of the Lune and eventually the Irish Sea. Every drop of rain, when such things came, would be sorted by gravity and the ground into left and right, eastwards and westwards, like water poured onto a rough dome.

Up at Nine Standards the view was enormous. Whenever I come to a great vantage point I always give a backwards look so that I can assimilate the past stretch and fix it forever with a single and comprehensive image; so that I can own it, as Beth's friends might (accurately) say. So I gazed back down into Swaledale and noted the steady height gains of the morning.

Then I did what the water does, and concentrated on the other direction. The prospect filled me with a new anxiety. It was not a feeling I had experienced before on this walk. It had nothing to do with the size and grandeur of the hills that were bulking up ahead, but something else. It did not take me long to realise what it was. The shapes to the north of me belonged to Cross Fell and Mickle Fell. To the south were the Mallerstang Hills. Therefore those ones ahead, away over on the far side of the Eden Valley, were Lake District Hills. I could probably even see High Street and Harter Fell, although the distance and slight haze were compressing that skyline into a single long serration. Now, if I could see those hills, it meant that the Shap Fells had arrived in the compass of my vision as well. And if that was the case, it meant that the little town also stood on this side of the horizon. So, therefore, did the narrow stone house, set slightly apart from the other buildings at the top of the town; and the old man inside it. All these things were folded into the mass of land before me.

I had to admit the old man had been right about the traverse. It was a far richer way of moving over the country than following a particular river or range of hills. I have often found myself drawn by the very routes I have decided against; yet the Pennine Way, dragging itself predictably up the middle of the map, held no attraction for me when our paths crossed briefly at Keld. Going across, the scenes change so dramatically that they and you catch each other unawares, and you go in a constant state of imminent surprise.

The anxiety climbed in me. I wandered for a few moments among the nine strange cairns. To the invading Scots they were supposed to have looked like an English encampment, and if you saw them at a distance from the floor of the Eden Valley, the theory was plausible. I would have liked something similar in my own journey - something that would alter from a deterrent to a folly as I came within range. Instead it was happening the other way round. The land ahead was full of stones. Barely thirty miles away now they formed themselves into a narrow building at the tip of a straggling town. To any other traveller it would be a presence of no significance, but to me it became more forbidding with each of my approaching steps. Of course I could still abort the journey. It would be quite easy. I would be at Kirkby Stephen by the evening. I would almost certainly have missed the last train out, but I could stay overnight at the Pennine or one of the other places that was too much of a hotel to be a proper pub and too much of a pub to be a proper hotel. Then the next day I could go up to the station, two miles from the town, and take the first train. If it went north I could go up to Carlisle and then off on the coastal loop that took for ever to get back down to Carnforth via Aspatria and St. Bees, Drigg and Millom. If it went south I could go over the Ribblehead Viaduct to Horton, and climb Pen-y-ghent. I could head up Langstrothdale Chase and, in getting lost, find some liberty again.

It was out of the question. The anxiety was there because the visit was of significance. Remove the trip, and the anxiety would give way to emptiness. I would reproach myself for having acquired the anxiety only to squander the energy of it.

Besides, there was Beth to think of. She would be angry for many reasons. All this time away from her without anything to show for it. I may not have known what she was expecting from the trip, but I was fairly sure she was expecting something.

I took the bridleway off from Nine Standards, with the view still ahead of me. Just as the land had tipped, so had the journey. It no longer concerned itself with departure but with arrival. I could once more feel the onset of shame and apology about my work. My father always judged a man by his work, just as he judged a woman by the extent of her support. Not that there should have been anything reprehensible about architecture. It could have been an awful lot worse than that. Design, for instance. Or any of the performing arts. They hardly bore thinking about. Yet he managed to get a down on architects, on the grounds that there were already quite enough buildings on the face of the earth. About twenty five years ago, somewhere between my qualifying and the last time we saw each other, he launched a furious attack on contemporary architects.

As ever, he took the practitioner before him - in this case me - as the one personally responsible for all the obscenities of the business. As far as I could gather, I had single-handedly stolen huge tracts of country, defaced river banks and obscured historic monuments with concrete boxes. It was an impressive achievement, given that low ambition and the recession had more or less pegged me to studio conversions in the Brondesbury area. I tried to tell him that he was charging me with the deeds of greater men, but he wasn't interested. I would have mentioned Lasdun, Rogers, Terry or various others, but it seemed hard on them, in their absence, to make them decoys in an irrelevant war. He always said I should have been a geologist and acquired a real knowledge of the ground. It was one of those remarks that I would rather have dismissed because it had come from him. But there was substance in it. Much as I love maps, there are times when I am sadly aware that theirs is largely a two-dimensional wisdom, and a mere chronicling of surface events. I would have loved to know the real stories - the assaults of moulten granite on the crust of the world, the buckling and faulting of the limestone and the squeezing-in of the ore veins. The stillness of the land lies on such strata of old violence.

The path now ran easily down Hartley Fell. It was the last stretch of the day, and the ground was good for striding. Before the quarries, and the village of Hartley, there was the steep cleft of Dukerdale on my left, with Rigg Beck in the bottom of it. The ground fell sharply down, three hundred or four hundred feet. I was aware of not wanting to look into that dip, and strode on even faster to put some distance between it and me.

Yer. Push. Yer. Push. It is too hard. A man should not push a woman like that, no matter what trouble there is between them. It is like one of those cruel, mismatched boxing bouts. To my surprise she is appealling to me for help, even though she does not know I am up here on the top landing.

Until this moment I have only seen the tops of their heads. Now her face is looking up at me. How can this be? Her arms are out imploringly. No, not imploringly. They are fighting the air for balance. Then I can see her front. She looks as if she is lying on her back. But this position is only held for a flashing instant before it all changes again. One of her legs kicks up, and then the other one. Her face is definitely looking at mine, and she is as alarmed as I am. She is going to say something. She has no contact with anything, and she is moving through the air on her back. This seems to go on for a long time, until she is near the foot of the house, and her head bounces off the wall, exactly like a football. Then it bounces out again into the middle of the flight, taking her body in its wake. A second ago her face was full of shock and outrage, but now there is no expression on it at all. More noises come from her head. The first two or three are very loud, just as you would expect from bone on sharp wooden edges. I can hear the acoustic of the staircase, just as if it is the body of a big instrument. The next ones are a little softer, probably because the worst of the falling is done and what she is doing now is more like bouncing down under the impetus. But then there is a different noise, the final one, and it is bone on the stone flags of the hall floor. After that, nothing but a shuffling kind of sound, which is the rest of her settling. When she has finished, and is completely still, the soles of her feet are looking back up at me. Between them I can see her body and, at the end of it, the underside of her nose, also looking back up at him, at us. I think there should at least be the sound of breathing out, because I am sure that she gasped when she was no longer attached to the ground, or when she saw me.

But there is nothing at all. Maybe all the air came out of her when the stairs thwacked her in the back. My father starts to go down. He is still saying "Yer," but his tone has changed. "Yer right?" he says. "Yer right?" I wonder if he also saw her looking up at me as she fell, because for no apparent reason he turns and looks up in my direction. As his head is turning towards me, I withdraw my own head from view, like a tortoise. At least I think I do, but I cannot be sure whether he has seen me or not. I lie there in the top of the house with my heart racing. I hear his heavy tread. Just for a second I think he has decided to come up, rather than go down, because the noise of the metal bits on the hollow stairs is so loud. But then I hear the footsteps grow softer as he goes to the foot of the house. He is talking to her again, quietly this time. He is calling her "love." I don't think I have ever heard him do that before.

"Best lie there for a moment, love. You'll be right." I wait for her voice. Even though the noises from her head were so loud, and the movement of it so violent, I am still expecting her to say something. Perhaps the argument will go away and they will speak politely to each other. She will say "Albert, don't let's have the sun go down on our anger," as I heard her say once before, in the kitchen, a long time ago now. But there is nothing. Just an isolated sound of him saying "Heck" beneath his breath, and the creaking and placing of his shoes on the hall floor.

I was striding on so fast that the next time I thought about where I was I had gone through Hartley and was nearly at Kirkby Stephen. Strange and disjointed pieces of information came back into my mind as the track reached the road and the road ran between the houses. Almost all the buildings here were made of brockram, which is limestone chippings in red sandstone cement. Also, a traveller writing in the 1830s had recalled arriving at the town and seeing a group of boys with a couple of men trying to bury a live horse. I had no idea where this had come from, and feared I might be imagining it.

I checked into one of the pub-hotels and then went to phone Beth. I didn't use the phone in my room, in the certainty that someone would listen in. I found a public box in the market square, but only got through to our answering machine. I had dinner, watched some television in an empty residents' lounge, and went early to bed. I meant to try and phone Beth again, but forgot.

Weeks later she told me that I had not wanted to phone that evening. I don't know what made her say it, but she was very sure about it. And I suppose she was right. It was something to do with what had been present in my head that afternoon, and my evident reluctance to tell her about it at that point. I don't know.

I slept, woke, half-slept and slept again, always with the sense of her in my arms. We moved through dreamscapes and unknown places, sensate exchanges and fragments of familiar talk. Sometimes she was the sex object that she had been for all the weeks between my first seeing her in the library, and my subsequent journey there when I knew, from watching the building, that she was inside. Then she was the woman I was living with, and our intercourse was domestic and reassuring. And then I was back in the wild places, thrilling and desolate, among shapes and motions that we had half-outlawed by our intimacy. It was tops and valleys, hard words and soft ones, shafts and ruts on heavenly flanks, and the flesh so much more giving than the ground. I would rather have been buried alive than have to hurt her as she had been hurt so badly before.

From time to time, in the growing hours, a tall figure stood in the room. First he was stony and admonishing. Then he seemed not to have seen me. And then he was stern again. Finally he was beaten into the air by the coming of the light.

I expected he would insist on remaining at my shoulder through the coming day, or else appear in formations of land up ahead of me. But he left me alone and I set off for Smardale, Severals, Sunbiggin, Oddendale and...Shap. The last one was non-negotiable, monsyllabic, final, like the last stop on a branch line. This stretch, over the limestone plateau of Westmorland, was my last twenty two miles. Like the leg from Keld to Kirkby Stephen, it was full of emptiness, if that is not too much of a contradiction. There were dead kilns and far older shapes, grassed over with fanciful christenings: the pillow-mounds, the Giants' Graves. In the case of Smardale the emptiness did fill the valley with a fine viaduct, which had made itself as indispensable to the character of the place as the famous one at Ribblehead. This one, taller and briefer, had once carried the railway that went from Tebay on the main line, all the way over to Darlington.

Set beside Severals, the line was a *parvenu*. The village covered about three acres, and I could just make out the traces of the dykes, holloways and field boundaries. Beyond it, up on Rayseat Pike, the ground remained cryptic. There was a particularly symmetry in a mound, and I assumed this was the longbarrow with a cremation trench. There was a skein of tracks, but I could not tell if they had been made by scavengers after stone or if they were the older routes of animals and human corpses.

"You'll wear your best suit for your mother," says my father. "There's a lad. Your Aunt Hilda's here to see to you, and you're to thank her properly."

His sister comes into the kitchen. She is the image of him: tall, gaunt, also about fifty, with indestructible shoes. If it is true that old women go manly and old men go womanly, then these two are going to be identical twins before they're done. Aunt Hilda has come down from Penrith. She has never married, and I can't imagine her ever lying down with a man inside her, and yelling with pleasure. Her top lip is crinkled and angry, like it is made to say no to all requests. I know she puts something chemical on it to stop a moustache growing. She has always hated my mother for marrying my father, and was glad there were such problems. She is trying to wear a sad face today, but it isn't working at all. "And then," she says, "when it's all done and everything has settled back down again, your father will take you on a treat. Isn't that right, Albert?"

"I don't know about a treat," says my father.

"You know," says Aunt Hilda. "What you were telling me about walking over the moors."

"That. Yes."

"It'll do you both the world of good."

Then we all go off in strange cars and bury my mother. She goes down so deep that I think she will never stop. People look at me as if there is something else going on. Something apart from the sorrow.

By Orton I had five miles to go. I had lunch there, but I cannot remember what I ate, or exactly where I ate it. Then there were four miles, and three, and two, but again that's about all I remember of the afternoon's walk. I can just recall being up on the scar and wishing its barrenness would go on for ever. Then I was at Lyvennet, then at Oddendale, aware of struggling to remember my phone conversation with Maud. But my memory had become wayward, and likely to take me into wrong directions. I still suspected that the wish for me to come here and see the old man was hers rather than his, and that she was trying to attribute it to him for some reason.

Then I was crossing the Mardendale Road and thinking of the time, away back in my boyhood, when there was no motorway between the village and here. You could get to this point by the paths across the fields. Soon I was high above the M6 traffic, looking down from the footbridge onto the roofs of roaring trucks and skimming cars. After my days among conduits that went in one direction only, this counter-driving was bewildering. The aggregate speed between two fast cars flashing past each other in their outside lanes was nearly two hundred miles per hour. Enough to cover in twenty five minutes the distance that had taken me four days. I stood on the bridge for a minute or two, watching the torrential power with which the great road tried to reassert the standard alignments of the country, from south to north and from north to south.

From here it was only a few hundred yards to the houses of Shap, with the railway running parallel. The two funnelled their way up through the gap in the land like strands of plug wire. Until the M6 came in 1970 the vital artery of the A6 ran right through the village. In fact you could say it was Shap High Street, stretched out long and thin by all the shops and cafes trying to get their fronts visible. At 1400 feet, and often deep in blizzards, it used to be a regular crisis point for families on holiday in their Ford Prefects and Standard Vanguards. My father would curse at the congestion and the (always southern) incompetence of the motorists. Then he would take a double-edged pleasure in going down from the house to help out with a jack-plug or a thermos of tea.

With the arrival of the motorway the village had lapsed into a backwater. I was away at college at the time, but when I returned soon afterwards I saw that it had gone backwards overnight. It had won a rebate from progress and become precisely the sort of quiet haven which most Englishmen yearn for in vain. I think it was when my father then fulminated against the motorway for taking local jobs away that I finally realised he was not a man to be pleased without a fight.

Soon after crossing the railway the lane came out into the main road next to the Kings Arms. I turned right and headed north. It would take no more than 10 or 15 minutes now to reach the end of the street and get the first sighting of the house, set back up its slight incline. I imagined the old man would be sitting at the downstairs window. The shops had shut down for the day and the pubs had not yet opened. A dog was crossing the empty road. Last year, when Beth and I were watching Psycho, she said how my description of the old house and the bypassed village reminded her of the Bates' home.

"Your young legs will make light work of the moors," says my father as we start from Robin Hood's Bay. And that is just about all he says all day, although he keeps looking at me as if he wants to ask me something. He doesn't know how well I can see him from the corner of my eye. Perhaps he is wanting me to ask him something. The next day, just as we are nearing the Lion Inn, he starts talking about the ironstone railway that goes over the moors from Rosedale. He talks so well, and with such enthusiasm, that I wish there were no other shared matters between us but this.

There was a call box near the top end of Shap. I made a mental note of it for phoning Beth later. I did not want to do so now. My reasons were all the usual ones of fearing the uncanny accuracy with which she could read my voice. Also, I was not too keen for more of the Inner Child stuff at the moment. After the dialogues of the day, it seemed that while it was I who had come to see my father, he was in some way already coming for me across the country and we were condemned to go round for ever in each other's footsteps. This last thought struck me as a sure path to despair and madness. I stopped for a moment to clear it from my head. I was terrified that the action of walking would make it reappear, rather as a return to sleep can re-awaken a nightmare. I took a few more steps and found that nothing filled my head except the sensation of being on rising ground, and the sight of a woman in black moving across the room behind my father's window. I had often wondered how my mother would have aged; whether drink and my father would have drained the life out of each other and they would have ended up circling like exhausted boxers in the closing rounds. And I had wondered whether they would at last have accorded each other the respect which opponents can share for the mere fact of having endured so long and kept the conflict alive. Like George and Martha in *Who's Afraid of Virginia Woolf.* Or Edgar and Alice in *The Dance of Death*.

These thoughts were dispelled by the opening of the front door while I was still several yards from the house. Maud was standing there, having seen me from the front room. She was a tall, erect woman, although obviously not as tall as she had appeared to a 12-year-old boy. She still wore her hair pulled back from the forehead, as all the sisters had done in the store. By my calculations she must have been about seventy, still nearly a generation down from my father. The set of her face made me remember the mixed smells of that place - the open trays of liquorice shapes, the magazines, the cold meats. I must have passed it on the way up, just now, and it must have turned into something unrecognisable in the long years of my absence.

"I expect it's all changed rather a lot," she said. She sounded slightly more formal, more confident than I remembered. Maybe she had grown like this as a result of living with my father and his sense of social position. It was a step up from weighing out quarter pounds of sherbert lemons for boys after school, and being silently looked down on as a refugee from the flooded valley.

Then she asked if I had had a good trip, and I found myself replying that I had walked. I was aware of sounding like someone who had got fed up with waiting for a train and struck out on foot.

"But not from London," she said.

"No, not from London. From Danby."

"Aha. Is that a very long way?"

It was turning into the kind of conversation that members of the royal family have with people whose lives quite escape them.

"Oh, about ninety miles."

"Actually," she said, "I do remember you saying you would be doing some walking before you arrived here. I'm sorry. Your father of course is a great walker."

I could see her studying me in return, and presumably trying to edit the adultness away from my face so that she could see the boy at the counter. Behind her shoulder, deep in the hall, I saw a tall dark mass. My eyes, still tuned to the light and the hills, were telling me it was my father, working his way slowly from the kitchen.

But it was a grandfather clock. I had not seen it before and took it to be a family piece of Maud's that had moved in when she did. It looked complacent and well in, more so than Maud. My eyes came back down the hall flagstones as far as the foot of the wooden stairs. The floor was too cold and the flight too steep to expect a woman to lie there with her legs up and her shoulders down.

"Do come in," said Maud. "You must be exhausted."

I walked in and caught the musty old smell of wood and stone. It was overlaid with something sweeter than when I had lived here, and I decided that Maud must be using a different wax polish to my mother's. This one was high and strong. It had only been recently applied, perhaps for my benefit.

A few of the pictures on the wall were the same as before, with the old line drawing of Helvellyn viewed from Patterdale still in pride of place. But the photo of the two them - I mean my parents - as a young couple outside the hotel at Wasdale Head had gone. In its place was a photo of a young family with lots of girls in summer dresses. They were standing next to a pub called the Dun Bull. As I knew that to be the name of the pub that had stood in Mardale before the flooding, I realised that the girls were Maud and her sisters.

It was odd to find these items of her life set out here in the spaces of my own past. Beth would ask me how it felt, and I would not be able to tell her.

"He's in the kitchen," said Maud. "You'd best come through." As I followed her down the hall she called out, "He's here, Albert."

I went in and there he was. He was sitting in the chair my mother used to sit in with her glass while he was out at work. When he saw me he looked as if he was about to stand, pushing himself up with his hands on the arms of the chair. I remembered the jacket. Brown course tweed. It had been his best casual wear when it was just back from Kendal, or wherever he'd got it. His flagship jacket. I don't think he ever did let on where it had come from. It might well have been Kendal. There were plenty of men's clothing shops there. And he might have kept it a secret just so as not to divulge his tastes too cheaply. Anyway, it was far sparer now around the shoulders and elbows, and it had lost all the eager stiffness of its youth. Although he had been expecting me for days, that half-raising of himself was the gesture of a man taken by surprise. Maud touched him on the shoulder and he sank down again.

He continued looking at me quite hard, just as I was probably doing back. I was waiting for the admonition to come into his eyes. I had no idea why it should, except that it always did. He never had a problem coming up with a reason. In the end it was not admonition that came, but anxiety. It might have been there all along, but I had never identified it as such. Now it was standing so deeply in his face that any frontal expressions of pain or pleasure would not have been able to erase it.

"So you've done it your old father's way," he said eventually.

"Well some of it, yes," I replied.

Maud looked on with her hands in a brittle clasp and glanced back and forwards between us as we spoke. I wondered if there was some terrible exchange which she feared would occur between us, and if she had been playing it over and over again in her imagination. More than that, I wondered what she knew about my father. Or about her predecessor in the house, apart from the facts that had become obvious by the end. The drinking, the misery, the dying.

"You remember Maud, don't you," he said.

Maud and I looked at each other. She smiled and I nodded.

"And how far did you come in the end?" he asked.

"From the Lion Inn," I said.

"At Danby. Where we stopped off that time."

"That's right."

"That was a grand break. So you'll have been over the Clevelands and the vale, and then the Dales and the plateau."

He was listing the features as much for his own benefit as for mine. I could see him logging the distances.

"And you've taken how long?"

"Four days."

He nodded.

"I'm not the walker I used to be," he said.

"Don't believe him," said Maud.

I sat at the opposite end of the table. Maud brought tea and sat between us. To my dismay a silence was falling on us. It was not like the old silences, it's true, as it was broken by the thudding tick of Maud's clock from the hall. I felt the start of panic. If silence was declaring itself so early as the currency of the visit, I might never find out why I had come. I would spend a few days here - the exact duration had never been discussed - and go away no wiser. They would wait for me to say whatever it was they were hoping to hear, or to not hear. Then I would leave, and they would make of it what they would. I still did not even know if they had ever married, and therefore if she was my stepmother. I reckoned that they probably had, as they would not have had the neck to cohabit. They were too old for that, too mindful of the town's opinion. But it would have been a quiet, invisible affair one morning at the register office in Kendal.

The more the communication between my father and me had rusted over the years, the harder it became to ask such basic questions. I could always go into the village, find a shop where I would not be recognised, and ask what had become of the old man up in the end house. When I looked at him he might have been fifty and me twelve, and the two of us proceeding for hours and days and miles without a word.

Maud's face seemed to be full of unexpressed intentions. Beth would tell me that I should just speak plainly to the woman, even though I barely knew her, and ask what was on her mind. That approach had a lot to be said for it, but since Beth did not know my pre-occupations and memories, she could not appreciate the complexity of the situation.

We drank our tea. Someone's stomach gave a long rumble. I found myself wanting to hear a little of my father's ill-will. A complaint or two. If he was going for the serene, butter-wouldn't-melt look in his old age, I would consider it an outrage. So many of them seem to do it at his time of life. I suppose they are taken in by this new frailty of theirs and pass themselves off as meekness incarnate. I decided it was time for me to test him out with references to way marking, television, the Boundaries Commission, or any of the other topics once guaranteed to raise the curmudgeon in him.

In the end I didn't have to bother. Unbidden, he said: "The vale, though. That's a dull dog of a place, isn't it." And then he was into his stride. I listened, as if for the first time, and Maud smiled broadly, like a nurse who can see the patient has got his spirits back.

After about half an hour he got up to go the lavatory. Maud shifted in her own chair. She obviously did this whenever he got up, and he, just as obviously, shunned her offers of help. The lavatory was on the first floor, which meant he had to get himself up and down that first steep wooden flight. I could hear him start to climb, the metal bits of his soles striking loud on the bare steps.

Maud looked at me. I suspected she wanted to use this brief absence of his to communicate something to me. But she only smiled again. I think she knew how hard I was finding it, even if she could not know precisely how my memory was peopling this house and its spaces. So I said: "My father seems well."

"He does," she replied. "Considering."

"Yes?"

"His age. Only that."

"Of course."

There was another silence and we could hear the metal tread arrive above our heads. We exchanged a few impersonal words about work, London, cars and the countryside. Then she leant forwards across the table and lowered her voice as if she would be frightened by his reaction to what she was about to say.

"Sometimes though," she said. "Sometimes I do get a little concerned. About your father. "

I tried to say something about how lucky he was that there was someone around to get a little concerned about him, but it didn't come out properly. She probably didn't understand a word of it but assumed that the fault was hers rather than mine.

"There's something he keeps saying," she continued.

"What sort of something?"

"It's probably very silly of me to even mention it, as I'm sure it doesn't amount to anything."

"It's not silly of you at all," I said. I had, naturally, been quite prepared to dislike the woman, but there was turning out to be a shortage of grounds.

"He has kept saying it of late. Well, two things actually."

"Two things."

"And always in his sleep. Agitated though."

"And what are these things?" I was trying to sound reassuring, like Beth can.

From overhead there was the sound of his shoes moving again, and the muted roar of the cistern. It was the same cistern as always, carrying on in good order.

"One of them sounds like 'Up off there,' or 'Get up off there.' It does change a little."

"And the other one?"

"The other one is...but you won't let on to him, will you?"

I promised that I wouldn't.

"Well, the other one is like 'Down from there.' Or else 'You come down from there.' It's quite difficult to hear properly sometimes."

"And always in his sleep?"

"Yes. I have gone in a couple of times and tried to ask him. Get him into a conversation. But it never works and he just says it again. He used to climb, didn't he?"

I replied that he did, and she said "As I thought." From having looked dark-eyed and anxious a minute ago, she became brisk and matter-of-fact. "It's probably to do with that. Giving instructions on a rock face."

I could hear his tread at the top of the stairs, and the familiar creaking sequence of the steps as he came slowly down. Maud waved her hand across the table to show that the subject was to be changed, and that it was not a particularly important subject anyway.

"I see that the drought is taking Haweswater right down," I said. I should have considered the sensitivity of this to her, but I was anxious to get on with a conversation, and used the first topic that came into my head. She didn't seem to mind, and said "Yes. It amazes me that people really believe a church spire is going to come up out of the water, and a village green and I don't know what else."

"Ah," said my father as he came into the room. "You'll be talking about Mardale. What a scandal that was. Decent folk with no grievances, and then that." I guessed he was still giving no thought to the linkage between Mardale's loss and his own gain. And Maud would have been too unassuming to point it out to him. Still, Mardale was a good cue for the old man's larger inventory of local outrages. As ever, he took it, and for the time being this removed the burden of conversation from us.

The real trouble happened deep in the night. I should have known it would. Looking back now, I must have been a little mad to sleep in the house. I could easily have got a Bed and Breakfast in the village. I suppose I must have worried about offending Maud. Of course Beth says that on one level (sometimes I dread that phrase) I must have wanted to stay, or else I would have gone elsewhere. Anyway, Maud gave me my old bedroom at the top of the house, saying I would feel at home there. I believe she meant well, but she could not have been further from the truth. Even while I was climbing the lower flight of stairs I knew I was going up into a lair of nightmares. They had been waiting for me all this time, as thick as cobwebs.

Before I reached the first landing I swear I could feel something tangle around my ankles. I couldn't tell whether it was trying to prevent me from climbing or to save itself from falling. Its grip proved weak, like loose seaweed on a swimmer's toes, and it fell away. Then, on the first landing, I had the sense of being jostled, and had to steady myself against the wall. I am not suggesting the place was haunted. Even committing that word to paper makes it look as though I was considering the possibility. But I was not, and nor have I done so since.

When I got to the landing at the top of the house I tried not to look back down. As I did so I knew it was foolish, but I was unable to stop myself. This meant that the last image I took with me into my room was the landing onto which I had looked down at my parents' heads.

My room had not changed at all. Even the counterpane on the bed was the same. It was quite likely that no-one had slept here since me, unless Aunt Hilda had come down from Penrith to see what her brother had got this time in the way of a woman. I was aware that sleep was a dangerous place to go, but I had no alternative. I had not only done a twenty two-mile day, but also found I was full of deferred exhaustion from all the anticipation of being here.

There was a hopeless sort of defiance in me as sleep gathered round like a town. I would see what was there. In the very last seconds of consciousness I thought I could hear my mother coming up the stairs. First the lower flight, hollow and distant, the pause on the landing, and then the top flight, close and loud. She would have leant over the bed, gently stroked my temple, smiled the soft and beautiful smile that she used to have so long ago before her breath smelled odd and her eyes were red, and then left me sleeping like a child.

Everything happened very quickly. The view from the top landing wasted no time in presenting itself to me. And there, just as before, were my parents' heads. They were bobbing backwards and forwards like string puppets, and there was a stark inevitability about what was going to happen next. There was the head, and there was the space into which it had to fall. I was yelling at the top of my lungs, but could not be heard. The head duly rotated into an upturned face, the shoulders turned like a page to reveal an outspread body, the legs kicked up from the edge of the landing, and then down it all went, soundless as mime, against that vertical backdrop. The expression went blank, the body bumped and slumped, and then the other head, my father's, turned to look up in my direction. I suppose it was at this point that my shouts became audible. I was calling out "Get up! Get up from there!" I was repeating it over and over again. I woke up with the noise of my own voice and found myself sitting up in bed, unable to stop calling. I put my hand over my mouth, but still the shouting went on, like an undying echo. It was no longer coming from me but from some other point in the house. I flung the bedroom door open, walked down the passage and peered down onto the middle landing. A dim light had been left on and I could see the figure of my father, gaunt and pale in his pyjamas, coming from the door of his bedroom. He grasped the banister of the landing and from the dark hole of his old mouth he called again: "Up from there!" Then the next door opened and Maud came out, hurriedly tying the cord of her dressing gown. As she raised her arms gently to touch his shoulders, I shouted "Look out!" as loud as I could. Both their faces turned to look up directly into mine, and my father bawled, "You come down from up there!"

In the morning I went into the kitchen and found my father sitting at the table as if nothing had happened. He was reading the paper and tutting at some piece of civic idiocy. There was a smell of fresh ground coffee, and Maud was busy at the stove. She smiled breezily and asked me if I had slept well. I looked at her to see if there was any irony in her face, any suggestion of a pact between us, but there was none. If a pact existed it was between her and my father. I am fairly certain that he had no recall of shouting on the landing, and that she was blanking it out in sympathy. Collective denial, Beth would call it. But then as far as I can gather everyone is in denial of something these days. I was once having an argument (it was either about smoking or Clint Eastwood) with one of Beth's friends. She said I was angry, I said I was passionate, and she concluded that I was in denial.

Anyway, when I realised that the events of the previous night were not going to feature in the breakfast conversation, I settled into that reality and buttered some toast.

"Will you be walking while you're here?" asked my father.

"Well I've done a fair bit to get here, you know," I replied.

"Aye, but I meant proper walking."

"I was thinking of taking him for a little drive around," said Maud. She looked at me with quiet determination for a yes, and I replied that I would like that very much.

"Drive?" said my father. "What d'you want to drive for? There's enough doing it as it is. You've both legs on you."

"I thought he'd be interested to see some of the old places," said Maud.

"Well, he'll find nothing has improved."

After breakfast Maud and I set off in her old Fiat. It was yet another very hot day, even at nine thirty. We drove past Shap Abbey, through Rosgill and on towards Bampton Grange. By now it seemed inevitable that we were heading for Mardale, although neither of us had mentioned it. When we came to the left hand turn for Burnbanks, the village at the near end of Haweswater, she said: "Do you mind if we take a look?"

I said I was going to ask her if we could, and was hoping she wouldn't mind.

"You've better manners than your father," she said.

"I don't think that would be too hard."

"Now where's that filial loyalty? she asked with a slight laugh. Then she added, very cryptically I thought: "No, you don't have to answer that."

We drove in silence onto the Mardale road, passing the dam on our right. Even in the bigness of the hills it was too large for its environment. One of the evacuated villagers once told my father that its concrete bulk had fallen on the valley like a final curtain. My father subsequently used the phrase many times, but always made sure of crediting his source.

"He won't come up here any more, you know," said Maud. "He swore he never would again, and he never has."

"That's my father. But then he doesn't really need to, does he?"

"Why's that?"

"Well, because you came down to Shap."

"Oh yes, I see what you mean."

The road stayed close to the water. The valley reminded me a little of Wasdale, over on the other side of the Lake District: a metalled road up the left, the real wildness in the hills across the water, and a dead end up ahead. Our route was as much of a corpse road, in its own way, as any of the old fell tracks, for it was built to compensate for the one that had run along the valley bottom before the flooding.

"You know," said Maud after another silence, "there's far worse things that happen, when you think about it."

"Worse than what?" I asked. My mind was on other things, and the question seemed to surprise her.

"Well, worse than Mardale. There was a great fuss about it at the time, but, well. Folks must have their water, mustn't they. It isn't fair otherwise. Not that I'd go around saying that. At least, not in a certain person's hearing!"

All around the lake edges were the low water marks that I had seen in the newspaper at Danby Wiske. That seemed like a very long time ago. Now those rims had grown into a broad ribbon beneath the edges of the surrounding land. Then, as we came up into the valley head, I could see how much further the level had fallen to expose the reservoir bed. Maud left the Fiat in the hotel car-park. I could feel a slight hurry in her movements, as though she was worried that a freak downpour would come this very moment and repeat the flooding. We walked back over the road and down onto the dry floor of the lake.

There was a peculiar scent in the air, and the ground stretching away beneath our feet was rusty and hard. Both the smell and the colour of the place were tropical. The walls looked engrained with dust, and the severed trunks of trees still clawed into the ground like desperate hands. Sheep were making a dry crossing between the peninsular known as the Rigg and the opposite bank.

With that great shawl of water slipping and slipping, a huge swathe of the old field system had been exposed. The little lanes meandered carelessly between their undamaged sides as if nothing had happened this past half-century. Even the Chapel Bridge, which Maud said was three hundred years old, was still standing there astride the broad stream-bed. There were two larger mounds of stones in what had been the heart of the community. These were the remnants of the little church and the Dun Bull - the sacred and the profane still huddling close, still making common cause in the English village of oblivion. They had been blown up and taken apart. Every scrap of wood - the doors, lintels, wainscots - had been removed so that they would not clog the filters when the water came up.

Maud had wandered a few yards on in the direction of the lake edge. She was peering from side to side, like someone not quite believing what she sees. Or not wanting to believe it. I think she must have seen some part of where she used to live - a twist in the ground, or the corner of a field. The expression on her face was reminding me of someone. It was wistful and resigned, with eyes that dipped between glances. My mother. It was the same look that my mother used to have when she studied her drink beneath its surface. I tried to recapture her image from the time before the perpetual dowsing of herself, but all I could reach was her face tipping back and dropping towards silence.

Maud walked back towards me. Her steps sounded hollow in the barrenness. I thought she looked moist around the eyes, and I turned my head away.

She said "No, it's all right," and when I looked at her again she was fixing me so hard with a stare that I couldn't look away. It was in no way hostile, but it was intense. I made what I thought was a questioning face in return, but it had no effect on hers. She stood still, focusing hard on me. We might have exchanged words at this point, but I don't think we did. Those few moments have become empty and unlogged, like the bare land to the west of Keld. The more I think about it, the more I believe we did not actually say anything. But we might have done. What might we have said to each other at that point, there in the dead trough of the lake? Not a day has passed since then without my thinking of such a conversation. It was as if time and place were suspended by the removal of the water; as if anything that we said would have been safe because any day now the level would rise again and take away the spot of ground where words had gone between us. What might we have said? That look of hers was inviting questions, and I guess mine was doing the same. What might our exchange have been?

Maud: "We know, don't we?"

Me: "Know what?"

Maud: "About what happened. Between them."

There is a pause. She is still staring at me so hard. It has turned into a look that could force your private opinions, your secret beliefs out into view by the power of its bore. I might say: "Yes, we know what happened. She was a terrible drunk." Or I might say: "Yes we know what happened. He pushed her to her death." I try to see which version she would rather have from me. But looking back at her, I realise that I don't know what she knows. And since I don't know that, I also don't know what else she might want to know. What does she tell herself when she is alone? Does she tell herself she is married to a man who was widowed by alcohol, or does she tell herself she is married to a man who killed his wife and got away with it? Does she want to know where I stand on the matter? Does she want to know if I am safe? Is that what I am really doing here?

As I keep telling myself, I don't think any of these conversations occurred. Yet some nights, even now, I am in them, in my sleep, and I wake from them as if I am being evicted from where I don't belong. They follow me into half-awakeness, still insisting on their reality and their immediacy. Sometimes she makes a remark with a platitude in it, about letting sleeping dogs lie or least said soonest mended, and gives me a conspiratorial little grin. Sometimes there is no shaft of inquiry coming out of her face, but only a look of utter terror, as if she is staring at someone who has the power to wreck her life, even at this stage. If I am sure of anything, it is that there was some sort of commerce between us in that dead market place, even if it was nothing more than a trading of silences on these terrible old subjects.

We were almost at Bampton Grange before she spoke again. She half-glanced at me from the driving seat and said "It must have been hard." Rather than asking her exactly what she was referring to, I made an agreeing noise and nodded. A little further on she gave me another half-glance and said, "You know, I do love your father."

It did not surprise me to hear her say this. It was obvious from her behaviour towards him. What did surprise me was that I offered no disagreement when she followed the remark by saying, "So we have that in common."

It made me think. It's not quite that I hate him. It's not as simple as that. I come from him and fear beyond words our involuntary pursuit of each other. When this fear is at its worst I feel my limbs turning to stone with the weight of his lived-out life, his opinions, his choices, his actions.

Maud parked in front of the house and said, "Remember now, no mention of where we've been."

When I got out of the car I could see him sitting on his chair in the front room, facing the window. I would have said he was looking out, except that he wasn't in a condition to look anywhere. His head had fallen onto his chest, and his arms hung limply at either side. He was quite clearly dead. It was typical of him. Two people start to discuss him in his absence and he upstages them both in the ultimate way. I now knew why I had been asked to come and see him at this time; he must have had a warning shot or two from his heart, and wanted to exercise his prerogative one last time over the family - meaning me. Now I would have to stay up for the funeral, which would be conducted by that same lugubrious family from Kendal. There would be an obituary in the *Gazette*, praising the courage with which he had faced the tragic loss of his wife. Perhaps Maud and I could begin to speak freely after all. This might mean the beginning of a liberty I had always lacked, or it might mean the onset of a remorse I had never expected. It was too early to say. How had he left his affairs? Were she and I to find ourselves on a collision course over money and property? One thing you had to concede about the old man. He did know how to get himself off the hook.

I drew Maud's attention to him, and she took it remarkably calmly. She went into the house and turned left into the front room.

"Albert," she said. It was a matter-of-fact delivery, and she could have been addressing it to him, to me, or to herself.

"Who is it?" he snorted, waking up with a jolt. His chin pulled away from his chest and his arms snapped back into life. "Oh, it's you. Where've you been?"

"Just down to Kendal and that," said Maud. And then to me: "He's always sneaking a quick snooze in when he thinks I won't know. Isn't that right, Albert?"

"There's rain due," he said by way of a reply.

"Does it say on the forecast?"

"If it said on the forecast, then I'd know we were in for more drought. No, no, I've the feeling of it."

"You should set up as one of those television weathermen, Albert. Don't you think? That would be grand I'd say, 'And now we're going over to Albert in the

Weather Centre.' And there you are, with your coat and breeches - oh, and a flat cap for outdoors - standing by the map, shovelling your little plastic clouds on and going 'There's rain due, I've the feeling of it.' Don't you think, Albert? Eh?"

She had started to laugh in the middle of her fantasy, and by the end she was losing control. Between these gusts of mirth she would repeat "I've the feeling of it," once even putting her hand on her head to indicate a flat cap. I couldn't quite believe what I was seeing. She had not struck me as a woman who might go skittish and do a turn. More to the point, I would never have thought that my father would tolerate being the butt of such a turn. On both counts I was wrong. A tiny motion started up at the front of his mouth and affected at least an inch of cheek on either side. It definitely qualified as a grin. It was even a slightly happy grin, and the more she laughed the broader it grew. When it was approaching medium size he noticed my puzzled look and called the sides of his mouth back in.

"You have to laugh, don't you," said Maud. I could not tell whether it was our conversation - rather, our lack of conversation - on the lake bed that had put her in such a light-hearted mood, or whether they were often like this with each other. After all, it was their marriage, or partnership, and you can never really tell what goes on in other people's unions. You think you can, but it is always wrong. There is always some small but crucial detail that you overlook. I tried to remember any skittishness there might have been between my parents in the days before they became so morose with each other and with themselves, but I could not.

"You have to laugh," said Maud again.

"And I don't see anything that's stopping you," said my father. He was looking a little uneasy now. He had displayed quite enough levity for one day.

Late that night the forecasters came in on his coat-tails and predicted rain. They got in just in time. The following morning a huge grey regiment of clouds came thundering in from the coast to liberate the land from the grip of drought. It had been developing its tricks during the long months of idleness and let off some peels that went right over the horizon and then came back up the other side of the world. The low trees on the fell swayed away in readiness. Rain drops came down the size of marbles and kicked up the dust in puffs. The ground gave off a smell of relief that was as sweet as first love. It was so fresh that it convinced you there had never been one like it before. I caught it through the open windows, and the beauty of it made me ache. I found myself thinking of Beth, and was glad of that. Perhaps I would suggest marriage when I got back to London. She had said that sort of thing wasn't important to her as it was really a step you took for the sake of children.

The three of us sat in the kitchen as the curtain of rain gathered around us. Its sound was music, conversation, vindication, and my father sat back at the head of the table with a look of profound satisfaction. Maud looked at him and smiled, and then turned to me. As she did so, she modified the smile. It was still warm, but it searched and projected, a little like her look the previous day beside the stone carcasses of Mardale. Again I returned it as best I could, and again I felt I had been inducted into a soundless conversation. In this exchange she was saying that the headwaters would be swelling from the slopes of Kidsty Pike and would come gushing down the becks of Randale and Riggindale. I was sounding like Beth and asking her how that made her feel, and she was saying something light about how it was a good job she didn't live there any more.

The rain kept up all day. There was too much of it for the dry ground and it went cascading down onto the old A6. I tried to imagine the present look of all the places I had been in the course of the week: the moors soaking it up without a word; the lead-land letting it run down its armadillo sides into the Swale; the Nine Standards turning dark with the drenching; the lake at Mardale preparing to put the upstart past back in its place. My father didn't go into the front room that day, but stayed in the kitchen where he could keep an eye on the rain through two windows.

It was a Sunday, and Maud asked us both if we would like to go to church with her. I had the impression these invitations had some sort of ritual status between the two of them - her asking him if he wanted to come, and him saying he didn't. I said I would be glad to go with her. I did this partly out of curiosity and partly, I think, out of the wish to be contrary with my father.

I thought he was going to say something disparaging to me, but instead he looked at Maud and said: "I know what the young feller'll get up to." This was a reference to the vicar who, it turned out, was the same age as me. "I know just what he'll say. I caught him doing it in Kendal when there'd been a downpour and he was just a shaver. He'll be giving it another outing. *Song of Solomon*: 'Many waters cannot quench love, neither can the floods drown it.' You wait and see. Oh, and when he buries me - if he dares - he'll be quoting from that Browning woman."

"That's enough of that, Albert," said Maud.

She and I drove down to the church. The wipers slapped in double time and the inside of the windscreen kept steaming up within seconds of me palming it clear. "He's such a witty man, your father," she said.

"Yes," I said, as non-committal as I could make it.

"And kind. I don't think people realise that. He wouldn't have me working, you know."

"I thought you were in the store," I said.

"No, I mean after...after."

She grew self-conscious and dried up.

All her sisters seemed to be at the church. They and the rest of the congregation looked at me with half-recognition. A grim old freemason called Mr. Teague was playing *The Lord's My Shepherd* on the harmonium, and everyone was trying to pitch themselves into their good octave for the high notes that loomed.

The vicar said something about it being grand weather for arks, and how we all needed to adapt, like Noah, to the great challenges that God put before us, be they in the violence of the elements or in the turbulence of our own natures. Then, sure enough, he went into his little bit of Solomon, without troubling his flocks with a linking passage. "Many waters cannot squash love, neither can the floods drown it."

The following day I left. Neither Maud nor my father said I should, nor was there any particular coldness coming from them. The time was up and the three of us knew it. There may or may not have been some activity on the landing during the night. And I may or may not have had a vocal dream. I would learn nothing on these subjects from either of their expressions. Before Maud drove me down to Oxenholme for the train my father shook hands with me on the threshold. We knew with the same unspoken certainty that it would be our last time. As the car drove down from the house I caught sight of him in the rear-view mirror. He was standing motionless in the porch, like a creature camouflaged in its habitat.

On both sides of the road south the country had been washed clean and green by the rain of the previous day. The intense heat had gone from the air, and the names of the region, with their suffixes of water, beck and mere, began to make their old sense again. The drought would be a strange patch in the memory of the land. The waters would close over its head as the time rolled on, and the smell of it would grow ever more foreign.

We passed a signpost to Burneside, and I heard my mother's voice say: "Out the back of Kendal. You were seen on the Burneside road."

"And you'll not leave it so long next time," said Maud in the station car park.

"No," I said. I tried to give her a token kiss on the cheek before getting out of the car. Our faces kept dodging from side to side, like people on a pavement, and our mouths scraped accidentally. We both gave an embarrassed laugh and said goodbye.

I did not leave it so long next time. Less than a year later she rang me in West Hampstead and I knew immediately. "It's funny," she said. "He was sitting in the front room when I got back from the shops, just like he was when you and I had come back from the lake. And I said 'Albert,' just as I always did, but this time there was no answer."

I went up to Shap for the funeral. Maud was surrounded by her sisters. She was more distraught than I had expected and they held her softly in their midst. The long-faced family came up from Kendal to do the business, and I longed for them to lighten up. Aunt Hilda spirited herself down from Penrith and frightened people with her resemblance to the old man. The flood-vicar had a full church and my father, though out of sight and horizontal, was vindicated once more. "As Elizabeth Barrett Browning wrote: 'Knowledge by suffering entereth: And Life is perfected by Death.' "

Some of the congregation had been present at my mother's funeral. Still they looked at me expectantly, wondering thirty eight years on what knowledge I might have that the coroner lacked.

I heard someone say "great old fellow," someone else say "part of the place," and someone else say "real pillar."

Real pillar. It should have been his epitaph. No-one would come up with anything richer than that.

"Are you OK?" said Beth in bed.

It was dark, and I must have woken her up.

"I think so," I said.

"It's just that you kept saying to get up. 'Go on,' you said. 'Get up.' And it's three in the morning."

"I'm so sorry."

"It's OK. I thought maybe it's a dream."

"Yes," I said. "I'm sure you're right. A dream. I love you, Beth."

"Me too."

I rolled over towards her for the embrace of her legs, and sank my face into her hair and her shoulder. She could feel my heart thudding in the absence of space between us, and stroked the back of my neck, gently but purposefully.

This must have been six months ago, a few days after the funeral. There was a lot of lying awake then. Long, long sessions of it after we had made love. They were full of gaps and silences on my part, and patience on hers. I suppose she hoped my father's death might clear some line of communication. As it was around that time that I wrote some of this, she was right. Her friends in the group would talk about going back and feeling the pain, and this thought filled me with fear and confusion. I felt I was at last striding free from the old man, without the sense of him looming behind me and taking me over in his stride, or else waiting by the path up ahead and drawing me off into places that were not mine.

"Why would I have to go back, Beth?"

"I'm not saying you do."

"You don't, do you?"

"It depends what you mean."

It is coming up to Christmas. I hate this time for its endless darkness and false light. But I like the solstice for its knack of nipping in just before and setting the longer days in train. I am up in the little attic study at West Hampstead, with bits of paper all over the desk. I am much better ordered when I use a drawing board. There is a Christmas card from Maud. Jo and her baby are coming to spend Christmas with us. There is no information about the father, but her Inner Child, now her outer one, turned out to be a boy. I tried this joke on Beth and she said it was very unfunny. She asked me how I would like it if I knew nothing about my father, and I said it would have its advantages.

When I sit down to write, I do anything to put it off. The dreams are going away. There was one the other night with the sun coming up over the Lion Inn. It was at my back, trying to cast my father's shadow onto the ground ahead, but I was having none of it. I have been reading this over from the beginning, going round again in my own steps, catching up and meeting myself here, at this very point. I know the route that has brought me here, but it has taken me to the margin of the map and I have no more.

I can hear Beth on the foot of the attic stairs. An unexpected but familiar smell came up from the pages while I was reading. I noticed that at fairly regular intervals, twenty pages or so, there was a crease in the bottom corner as if it had been folded over to mark a place and then unfolded again as the reader resumed. There was one such fold at the Lion Inn passage, another when my account reached Danby Wiske, and then another at Reeth. It gave me the strange sense of observing my own stalker's track by the clues of flattened undergrowth. Then I came to the part where I am on the steep cleft of Dukerdale, with Rigg Beck at the bottom of it and me not wanting to look down. Yer. Push. The page was still folded at the corner and the scent was full and strong.

She is coming up behind me, shortening the distance at every step. Her tread is on the top stair. She is in the room. She will lean over me with her sweet breath, smile gently and stroke my temple. Later perhaps we.

THE TARN-ISHED MUSE

Wendy Howard-Watt glanced at the dashboard clock and put her foot down. The roadworks had squeezed the A44 into a single lane for miles to the south of Evesham. It was already a quarter to four and the compact bumps of the Malvern Hills had yet to appear on the skyline. Lady Templeton had suggested four so that Miss Howard-Watt - she had simply assumed her to be a miss - could have a spot of tea with her and Sir John. She promised her visitor she would then make herself scarce so that the two of them could get down to the business of the afternoon. She would find him, Lady Templeton assured her, in robust health, considering his great age. She could have an hour and a half with him, and should remember to speak up when she put her questions. He had refused all attempts to have him fitted with a hearing aid, and had become intolerant of people who did not project.

This was fine by Wendy. She had sung in the Schola Cantorum at Oxford, and played Cordelia in an open air production of *King Lear* at Balliol; as she generally let people know quite soon after meeting them. No problems about voice.

Only one other thing, said Lady Templeton genially. Better to stay off personal subjects. For example, she herself had "ruffled his feathers somewhat" by mentioning that it was his birthday the following month. Apart from that, anything went. She sounded like the curator of a national monument which, though structurally sound, was at no time to be clambered on.

At last the little line of hills appeared, a very old animal squatting down at the edge of England. There was its humping back and rear, and its forepaws tapering down into the level plain. Its presence was always a surprise. It shouldn't have been there but it was, and very fixedly so. As her geologist cousin Russell had once explained patiently to her while failing to seduce her, it was the oldest thing around by miles. It was the surrounding features that were the upstarts.

Wendy Howard-Watt was neither Miss nor Ms but Mrs. In this she was quite rare in her trade. It was the legacy of a strange arrangement she had made when agreeing to marry Guy. She would keep her own maiden name, dull and monosyllabic though it was, and put his, old and landed, on the front. And she would prefix it with Mrs., partly as a sop to his uxorious zeal, and partly to make it sound established, bedded down. Her sister said it made her sound like a series of questions, When? How? What?, and wondered if it was wise for someone to wear her pushiness quite so clearly on her sleeve. She ignored the sister, as she always had (who would want advice from a country parson's wife?), and put the quibble down to the old jealousy.

It was extraordinary how people never questioned the provenance of a double-barrelled name. They just took it as a token of class, whereas it might have been another kind of greed. As long as you maintained that first good impression by flattering the judgements of the commissioning editors and by seeming to know everyone who was on the brink of fame, the work came tumbling in. Then the by-line became more prominent, sometimes even carrying a mugshot. This was celebrity in its own right, and generated still more work. Wendy Howard-Watt went into the gardens of the wealthy and gawped through her prose at the topiary. Wendy Howard-Watt entered the homes of the famous and celebrated their formula for marital bliss. Quite soon no bathroom or toilet in certain parts of north London could be described as a total success without a visit and a public report by Wendy Howard-Watt.

The other great discovery was that if you were not nasty about people, then you would start getting calls from PRs who seemed to control the availability of some really very big names indeed. We are talking Markowitz, Pallow, Dimitri. We are looking at three days in the Chateau Marmont on Sunset, with WER picking up the tab. The only thing the client jibbed at, they would explain, was when the reporter tried to impose his or her own agenda. This did not go down well. And so Wendy Howard-Watt could gradually be found shooting the breeze with the Marcellis in Santa Barbara, and hanging with Mishi Brahms in Vegas. And if she wasn't entirely sure why these people meant so much to a certain sector, or articulated the fears of a particular generation, she had the grace not to let on. Let others make their names through nastiness. She had nailed her colours to the mast of compliance and the ship was billowing along handsomely with the wind of good opinions.

If she had ever privately despised an aspect of their work, she would talk herself round before the plane touched down at Burbank. Sure, she had had her doubts about Joey Rourke's psychotic cop-killing cop in *Streets of Meat*. However, just when she was going to raise the ethics of that undoubted genre classic during their two-hour exclusive in the penthouse suite at the Marmont, he - let us be very clear about this - shagged her.

No, she did not mention this in the piece, although heaven knows she could have written an award-winning account of the bedroom scene. And then she could have made this a kind of motif in all her interviews with men, keeping the readers guessing till the end. Wendy Howard-Watt pulls the stars. Redford? Suddenly so crumbly. Clinton? Wary these days. Spacey? A real challenge. She felt her mind slipping from the enclosure of acceptable thought.

This might have been brought on by her almost lateness and the onset of anger. It could well have been a mild case of road rage. Then she realised it was just her dull monthly visitor who seemed to come earlier each time. As usual it had barged in and plonked down its effects - the loopy thoughts, the nameless violence, the filthy ache and the odd smell of curry that came up form her collarbone. A curry flavoured with lead and anchovies. It never picked the right moment. That was part of its style. But this was singularly bad timing.

It was just as well she wasn't at home as Guy had taken to asking if she had PMT every time she said something offhand to him. It meant that in the only place where she felt able to express a hostile view about someone - her husband admittedly - she was told it didn't count. This was unacceptable. It assumed that her sharpness or her pissed-offness could always be explained away by her having the painters in. And where had he learnt that horrible expression anyway? Some men thought that just to mention the word, or letters, meant that they were modern and sympathetic. But in the end it was no different from her elderly father believing he proved his liberalism by saying the word Marxism matter-of-factly. Both men were going through the motions while remaining terrified of the concepts.

And another thing. If she had a period as often as Guy asked her if she had one, she would have been suffering from that illness which T.S. Eliot's wife had, when it never stops. Guy could be so dense. It was not even as if he was doing anything that might make her stop having periods. All that had very literally ground to a halt since he fell asleep on top of her, again, and woke up calling out her sister's name. A different sister this time, the little boyish one who was being such a handful, but a sister just the same.

It all probably played its part in the air of availability which the editors seemed to sense about her. In her most regular Sunday outlet they were using a photo that showed her as twinkly and questing. The accompanying standfirst would say "Wendy Howard-Watt gets to grips with an enigma of the airwaves," or "Rufus Dowling has an unmentionable problem. Wendy Howard-Watt gets on top of it."

One thing led to another, which in turn led to Malvern. Brenda Findlater, who had handled this type of interview for the paper for the past twenty years, was on a free trip to Paraguay. The Templeton window of opportunity had been opened suddenly and unexpectedly by the old man's agent, the waspish Harold Liss. The article would coincide with the publication of a coffee table book on Sir John's career. Brenda would be furious when she got back as she prided herself on being good with old people. She had at least three different ways of saying that they were national treasures. A long time ago she had generated record levels of correspondence by describing Barbara Cartland as the People's Queen Mother. The mere thought of Brenda's pique was a source of delight to Wendy. Like many others, she was less than convinced by Brenda, who had transparently married her way to the top. And it was important not to lose sight of the fact that she was, when it came down to it, fat.

The hills had come forward into the middle distance and now accounted for most of the view ahead. You could see the cleft to the north of Worcestershire Beacon, and pick out the browns and greens of autumn on its flanks. As ever, the town clustered at the foot, thinking about climbing a little higher but not being allowed up.

Wendy Howard-Watt on a grand old man of the English stage. No. Wendy Howard-Watt attends the first knight of the British theatre. No. In a rare interview Sir John Templeton reveals the secrets of his professional longevity and explains how he very nearly went into banking. ("I thought he had done," wrote one critic of his Prospero.) But then where would you put the by-line? In a rare interview with Wendy Howard-Watt Sir John Templeton reveals blah blah blah. No, that would make it sound as though the rarity was her doing the interview, which was very far from the case. Oh well. Sub-editors, the people who wrote the headlines, were actually more skilled than you thought, even though they were viewed as the pond life of the paper world; even though they were, with one or two exceptions, middle-aged men who smelled smoky and bitter and still wrote puns around Sixties pop song titles, and had not a single natural fibre in their wardrobes, and fancied her as much as they hated her, which was lots. One of the two exceptions was a shy young woman called Melanie Woolf. She was rather mousy but quite bright and seemed to have taken a friendly interest in Wendy. Most important, she was very complimentary about Wendy's copy and they had had a couple of good talks about writing. Good in the sense that it was clearly understood that Wendy was senior partner in the exchange of opinions.

She glanced down at the photocopied press cuttings on the passenger seat. She had had them biked round to her home in Camden the previous day and marked some relevant passages in bright felt-tip. Old-fashioned perhaps, but there was often information in cuttings which you still couldn't get off the net. The coverage went right back to before the war, down into the Thirties and Twenties and perilously close to the First War. After all, he had started as a child actor in companies you had never heard of. He had been a member of Billy Ball's Dewdrops, living away from home, tap-dancing his way around the old reps of the north.

Then it seems he was captured by aunts and forced into some sort of penal unit that passed itself off as a boarding school. He emerged from this with enough of an accent to land small parts in the classics: second soldier, first soldier, messenger, Mountjoy, and so on towards Young Hal's understudy for J.B. Denham. Pleurosy laid low the lead, on he went and the rest, as the cuttings kept saying, was history. Or rather, as Wendy Howard-Watt was going to say, Histories: *Henry Four* one and two, *Henry Five* and then, memorably, at Wyndhams, *Richard the Third*. Or as George Burns used to say, Dick Da Terd. After that the great American tour of the Scottish play. Or as Jack Benny used to say, Mac the Wife. And then, still ridiculously young, the famous London production of *King Lear* in which he became, by universal agreement, the Lear of his generation.

It struck Wendy that you only had to play Lear or Hamlet to be the Lear or Hamlet of your generation. To her certain knowledge there had been at least two of each in the Nineties alone. Robert Stephens and Ian Holm for Lear. Stephen Dillane and Ralph Fiennes for *Hamlet*. Not Kenneth Branagh though. He was a Hamlet for someone else's generation. She had met Branagh, but by that time he had been profiled once too often to be interested in her.

There was so much on Templeton. The tireless work for charity and the constant waiving of fees; the legendary courtesy to all sorts and conditions; the love affair and seventy-year marriage with Lady T.; the devotion that made her lay down her own career for a union which was to prove, sadly, childless; the magnanimity with which he stepped aside to let Gielgud direct himself in *He Was Born Gay* by Emlyn Williams at the Queen's in 1937. One could go on and on. The innumerable Chekhovs, Ibsens, Maughams, Shaws and Rattigans, distributed across the decades and the regions with all the good, tried taste of certain Englands at certain times, always long-suffering, always hopeful, always so impressed. And let no one forget how well he adapted - "re-invented himself" was the usual form of words - when the wave of young anger came and swept all the landmarks away in the Fifties. There was a churl who suggested that his appearance on this new stage was linked to his rejection by the old. It was probably Osborne, but Templeton had been as good as his word and outlived him, just as Osborne had once outlived himself. He was as old as the hills to which he had retired.

These now showed off their limited vastness and towered at Wendy through the windscreen. The road rose on the beginning of their gradient, and the view in the mirror fell back towards Tewksbury. Just time to give the cassette one last burst. It had been specially made for her drive down by Matthew, Guy's best and oldest friend from school and university. It was a recording of him pretending to be Sir John Templeton and regaling her with anecdotes from his career.

Matthew was an actor. Not a very good one, it had to be said. Guy and Wendy had stood by him, or rather sat by him for years, regularly swelling audiences by a hundred per cent for O'Neill revivals in the backrooms of unspeakable pubs near the Oval. However, he was a brilliant mimic. His best take-offs of famous actors were simply as good as it gets, and indistinguishable from the original. Thanks to a fresh and vicious job on Jonathan Ross, he was just getting the sniff of a Saturday night spot on Channel 4. Nothing in his repertoire could ever be better than his Templeton. If there was any criticism of it, it would be that because people assumed Templeton was dead there was not much of a market. No matter; the market of one at the wheel of the Saab would have bent double if the steering wheel had let her. Sir John was coming in stereo from her speakers, all splash and plum and pointless clarity. "Thish, d'you shee, wash back in the daysh of Harcourt Williamsh." Good old Matthew. She switched it off so that she could compose herself to meet the real thing.

She drove up St. Anne's Well Road as Lady Templeton had instructed. "Be warned, my dear, it feels as if you are driving into the sky." The motor was no fool and put itself at once into first gear. "Then right, off the tarmac and through the big white gate which we shall leave open for you."

As she swung right she glanced down at the tremendous view of fields, the slight smudge of Worcester to the north, and Bredon Hill standing forward like a stray Cotswold. Which role was England in today? Thing of rags and patches; rust-hued old trouper; land of infinite span?

More to the point, which role was Wendy Howard-Watt in? Heritage pilgrim; lifelong fan; arts crumpet? There was one other possibility which had dared not speak its name since she set out from Camden three hours ago. Yesterday evening she had spoken on the phone to an ancient aunt, Beatrice, her father's much older half-sister. Hearing that her clever niece was off to see John Templeton, she decided to tell her something that she had never told anyone else. It concerned an old school-friend of hers called Kitty, an actress. The two of them had shared a flat in Kensington shortly before the war. Kitty had had an affair with him while playing Hermione to his Leontes in *A Winter's Tale*. It had started at the Alhambra in Bradford and progressed all over the country to the Royal in Bath. Kitty fell in love with him, and he gave her to believe that he would leave his wife for her. In Salisbury Paulina noticed a change in her shape during the statue scene and Kitty confessed to being pregnant. When she told Templeton he ordered her to have it aborted.

"She was mad for him, dear," said Aunt Beatrice. "She'd have done anything for him. He was very dashing, Johnny Templeton. He told her that if she didn't lose the baby it would be the end of her career. Well, he was righter than he could have known because, to come to the point dear, she went to see a woman in Bristol and she not only lost the child's life but her own as well. I can never see that play now for fear of breaking up when Perdita comes back to life. Poor Kitty. Well, Johnny Templeton and the rest of the company put it about that she had got pregnant by a drunken stage-hand in Leeds, but I can tell you it wasn't so. There now. I've been wanting to tell someone that for years. Now you won't go printing all that, I know."

Wendy Howard-Watt tracks down sex-rat Templeton. Callous star "killed" mistress and love child.

"I wouldn't dream of it, Aunt Beatrice."

The car nosed into the drive and the gravel made the rich sound effect that was expected of it. There before her was a substantial house topped with an eccentric array of different sized gables. "This castle hath a pleasant seat. The air sweetly and nimbly commends itself to our something something. To our gentle senses." Shakespeare was so useful. Lady Templeton looked tiny against the high, broad frontage. She only seemed to come half way up the front door. Hello Lady Templeton. Goodness how you've shrunk. She rested one hand on the other and leant her head slightly to one side. It was a practised manner for receiving things - visitors, thanks, plaudits, groceries. She stepped forward and stood in the drive. Wendy rummaged her cuttings out of sight and got out to meet her.

"I say, well done you," said Lady Templeton. "Did it take you a very long time?"

"Oh no, not too bad at all."

"I'm afraid we're most dreadfully out of the way here."

"It is absolutely beautiful."

"Well you've certainly brought the nice weather with you."

"Have you lived here long?"

"Nearly eight years. Really since John finally called it a day. We used to come here when we were very much younger, and always talked of retiring here. And now here we are. So, not very adventurous I'm afraid. Do come in. John is upstairs with the photographer. I don't suppose they should be too long."

The photographer. She had forgotten about him. His name was Reg Brace and he lived in Redditch. He was a partner in an agency and regularly did work in this region for Wendy's editors. She had met him when she was doing that animations woman in Hereford. He looked like a porter, with camera straps that pulled his jacket off his shoulder. He always wanted longer with the interviewee than had been agreed, so that he could suck up to them and get things autographed. He considered the journalist a poacher on his time and assumed the feeling was mutual. In

Wendy's case he was spot on.

"Mr. Brace, who is a charming man, has come to take pictures of John several times since we've been here," said Lady Templeton. "Excellent photographs. Not that I am an expert in these things."

"Do you think he'll be long?" Wendy asked as mildly as she could.

"Oh I shouldn't think so. John's very easy."

"Only, I should hate to get in the way, or run over my time with your husband."

"Well that's very professional of you. Perhaps we can go up and put our noses in now, see what's doing and then I can show you round afterwards when John has his nap. I'm not letting you go back without a little tour."

"Thank you," said Wendy. "That would be lovely."

"But we won't hang onto you too long, as I'm sure you'll want to be getting home."

They walked up the broad staircase to the landing. The walls were densely hung with black and white photographs of young men in doublets, slightly less young ones in togas, and decidedly mature ones in solemn robes. You only needed to look once to see that they were all Sir John Templeton at different stages and in different guises. Each one had been diligently captioned with the role, the theatre and the date. Wendy Howard-Watt walks down the century with Sir John Templeton. No. Showgirl Shame Of Two-Timing Temples.

She was expecting a left turn along the landing into one of the bedrooms. Instead she found herself being led by Lady T. along a narrow passage that wound towards the back of the house. It went on for a long way, until Wendy realised they were heading for some rear room that must be an outcrop from the main building. In the final straight they ran into Reg Brace coming from the door at the far end. He was dabbing his brow and looked distracted.

"Ah, Mr. Brace," said Sir John's wife. "I expect you two know each other."

Brace was forming the face of a man about to give a valuable piece of advice for free. Then he looked at Wendy, remembered her from the Hereford animations job and his goodwill evaporated.

"That's right, we do," said Brace.

"And everything going well in there with John, is it?"

The photographer hesitated in his reply and eventually said "Fine thanks, Lady T." Then he turned to Wendy and said "All yours love," and passed on down the corridor. She could have sworn he was smirking about something.

Lady Templeton knocked on the door, opened it and put her head round. She projected the words "Miss. Wendy. Howard. Watt." in her best RADA voice before ushering the visitor in and withdrawing immediately.

Wendy heard the door shut behind her and found herself standing in a large area of polished wooden floor. Dotted across its expanse were little flecks of masking tape and groupings of chairs, apparently denoting characters. One bore a label saying Cassius, another Casca, a third Brutus. Of Britain's foremost exponent of classical technique however, there was still not a sign.

A voice - The Voice - repeated the three elements of her name like a deeper echo of his wife. Unhelpfully it made her think of the Noel Coward story she had heard the other night: "Nyree. Dawn. Porter: Three. Dreadful. Actresses."

The Voice came again. "When did he? How did he? What did he?" He was making her name sound like the inspector's lines in a melodrama. It was really quite sprightly for an old boy. This would make good colour for the piece. "He greets you, as it were, from the wings, a disembodied voice announcing to a patient house the imminent arrival of their idol." She turned her tape recorder on so as not to miss anything. When he finally appeared from behind the screen it was not his dignitas or his legendary presence that struck her, but the sheer size and vigour of his erection. The veins were standing out in a way she had never seen before - certainly not on Guy's. He looked as if he was riding it like a hobby horse across the bare floor, clip-clop, with his ankles half-hobbled by the fallen trousers.

He cried "Whoa!" into the thin air before him, but this did not bring him to a halt. One arm was raised and waving behind his shoulder, like a fencer's counterbalance. If pressed, Wendy would have to admit that nothing had fully prepared her for this. But then the unexpected was at the core of the job. Take the Chateau Marmont situation. Perhaps this was another one of those, although the old man did not seem to have noticed her. He let out more shouts and strange words, and at last wrestled himself to a standstill. Among his weird utterances she was sure she could hear him say "Who would have though the old man to have so much blood in him?"

Aha, so it was a jolly gambit, with a false thingy. Risqué certainly, but actually very modern when you thought about it. "The routine is in the mainstream tradition of matinee japes that litter the Templeton career like sudden clutches of confetti on stern moorland." No. What would they be doing there?

For a moment he looked as if he might be about to swivel and charge, an old beast at bay. Instead he stood rooted there and barked a few more strange oaths at his tumescence. One of them sounded like "Begone viper!" Then he watched in childlike wonder as it shrunk and vanished.

Wendy decided to carry on as if nothing had happened. She even allowed herself to think, or hope, that all this was some sort of manifestation thrown up by the madness of the month. She fumbled for her line about understudies and gave it a shot: "It's a funny thing, you know, I was just thinking on my way here, you got that crucial break when Prince Hal fell ill in 1928, and I can really identify with that because if a colleague of mine had not been away - well, not actually ill but in Paraguay - I would not have had the chance to be here now, talking to you."

This did not seem to be having the desired effect on Sir John. In fact it was having no effect at all. He simply looked ahead of him at some indeterminate point. It reminded her uncannily of Stephens' Lear at Stratford when, in the small gap between Cordelia's death and his own, he focuses on something that no one else can see. Had Stephens taken it from Templeton? Was Wendy Howard-Watt witnessing at the closest possible hand the colossal influence on those who came behind in his kinglike footsteps? Or was he simply about to die?

Wendy Howard-Watt is in at the death of a great Englishman.

It was not to be. If ever there was one who would move noisily to his close, full of alarums and excursions, this was he. We were in the final act of course, but the actual end would have a climb, a build, and in his single death would be embodied all the loss and moment of a Jacobean charnel-house finale. And you would get plenty of warning.

She could move straight into the question of his affair with Kitty Moncrieffe, Aunt Beatrice's friend. That might at least have the effect of making him realise that Wendy was there. "So tell me, Sir John, do you have her death on your conscience to this day, like any normal bloke would? After all, if you hadn't threatened the poor girl like that those two lives would never have been lost. Plus, by the way, you might well have had a son and heir."

What she eventually said, as loud as she could without appearing berserk, was: "You must be thrilled by the new book, Sir John."

He took a step back, like a stage soldier checked by a rapier thrust. His jaw was hanging open in contempt and disbelief.

"Must me no musts, woman. Are you with the company?"

She tried to reply that she was with the fastest-growing quality paper of its kind, not just that but with the most-read section of that paper, according to every single one of the latest focus groups, but he was not remotely interested. It was here that his behaviour went downhill. One could argue that until this point none of it had been personally slanted. Now all this changed.

"Yer King-Urinal, yer filthy bung," he boomed. His voice still had an astonishing force. "Yer scambling bawd, yer dunghill cur." His face locked into a gargoyle glare, with staring eyes and a dark absence for a mouth. Well, she told herself, it could still be play-acting. He had always been praised, and rightly, for the conviction of his vocal attack. And these phrases; they were actually very quaint. The readers would love this, being sworn at in Shakespearian.

Then this too changed, and Templeton brought himself resoundingly into the modern age. "Ya cunt. Ya scabby-twat cunt-whore. Ya come here. Ya take the flower of our, of our, of our, and ya blow it to siffy shards of bloodshit. Ya cunt."

For the next few minutes - hard to say exactly how long - he kept up a more or less continuous stream of abuse. Sometimes it delved back down into the harmless mud of Pish, Tush and pox; sometimes it would yoke them horribly with fresher and starker sounds and a mutation would emerge: "ya giddy-girdling wanker; ya tallow-blubbered arsehole." At one point Wendy tried to pitch herself between him and his words, and received three or four answers that sounded lucid enough. But then the torrent closed over her head again. Eventually his voice ran down and the words shifted from sustained attack to undirected litany. At last it came to rest and there was a large hollow silence in the room.

Wendy felt herself starting to cry. On this occasion there would be nothing strategic about the tears. In her mind's ear she could hear her commissioning editor tell her what she already knew: "Basically Wendy, it's unusable. Sorry, but there's really nothing here for us." Then she could hear one of the assistant commissioning editors saying to another: "The man is obviously ga-ga. That Howard-Watt woman should have done a few checks. Don't you think? I mean, you don't just go off to Monmouth or wherever it was and expect lucid wisdom from someone of that age. I've always thought she was a bit crap. I've never quite got what they see in her. Apart from the obvious."

Finally she could hear Brenda Findlater, back from Paraguay, revelling in the yarn and phoning people with no other purpose than to pass it on to them. The story would burgeon out of control, as such stories always did, until it featured Wendy trying to have Sir John on the floor of his studio and being rebuffed. "Can you imagine how humiliating? Being turned down by a ninety-something?"

While the tears seeped from her, slowly and quietly, Sir John retired to the far end of the room, sat on a canvas chair and dozed. He looked so blameless there, with his eyes closed and his hands folded across his chest, as peaceful as a brass rubbing. Age and repose were, in their own way, as unscrupulous agents as youth and beauty. They went to work on a subject and ironed the low intent from its features, the sin from its past. Teenage girls and ancient men could be equally blessed by their attentions. Young teases went unspotted and old love-rats went untrapped.

Wendy felt unable to move. There was a danger that fresh activity might set him off again. If this was not an isolated outburst, it was hard to imagine what his wife thought about it all and how she felt able to let anyone into his company without first warning them about him. She seemed such a balanced, thoughtful woman. And she was another reason for Wendy feeling stuck. If she went back downstairs now, after such a short time, it would be embarrassingly obvious that the interview had been what it was, a complete disaster.

She decided to re-wind the cassette and see if anything, anything at all, could be salvaged from the wreck. Although the old man's train of expletives was hardly going to be laid before the public on a two-page spread, there might be a fragment of something for the diary column. With the stuff they were printing these days, they must be desperate for tips. As she replayed the tape, the strange words sped past her ears again, with some more that she had not fully taken in at the first hearing. Clack-dish, bed-swerver, rank-scented meiny, vagrom men, trod-my-dames. Now that they were disembodied, while still having the benefit of his sonorous voice, they had a certain wonder. They were like old materials - loam, reddle, daub - and they were all pushed together into a coarse and makeshift elegy for a time that had become lost through no greater sin than lingering. Then she came to the part that she had forgotten about. Extraordinary how the memory could wipe things. It had happened just after a terrible bout of abuse. She must have responded to that with a sort of shock-deafness. Anyway, here was her own voice, edging bravely into a narrow gap and asking him what he had thought about Olivier.

"Olivier?" This was one word he evidently had no problem hearing.

"Thundering ham."

A little later she had managed to say Gielgud, and he had responded with "Simpering pansy."

Richardson?

"Never convincing."

Scofield?

"Promising."

But then back it went into that strange wild babble. If only she had persevered, really shouted at him, she might have got more in this vein. It did seem odd that he only became remotely normal when invited to disparage dead and former rivals. No matter. It had given her an idea. Some might say it was the best idea she had ever had in her professional life, although Some was not to be told about it.

After another decent interval she walked silently from the room, leaving Sir John asleep on his chair. She made her way towards the landing along the winding corridor. Downstairs Lady Templeton was on the lookout for her, and beckoned her into the kitchen. It was a vast low-ceilinged room with an old range and a dark flagged floor. Outside, above the incredible view, the day was warm and rounded. With the autumn light in the air and the leaves still on the trees, it had more gold than it knew how to use and was offering it round to every part of the landscape that was interested. All the smells were on the brink of turning with the year and spicing the taste of vague remorse. There was a sweet wood scent from an open grate in another room. The years were banked up as nobly in the stones of the building as they were in the bones of its presiding pair. England didn't get much better than this. The only thing that marred it was the sight of Reg Brace being persona grata at the kitchen table.

"Thank you, Lady T. I won't say no."

He looked up as Wendy came into the room, hoping to see the signs of advanced distress on her face. He was to be disappointed. With the idea now rooting and fruiting in her head, she had composed herself.

"So," said Lady Templeton. "Everything all right?"

"Absolutely," said Wendy. "I'm terribly grateful to you for having me here. It's been truly fascinating."

"He is rather good value when he gets going, isn't he, although as his wife I suppose I'm bound to say that, aren't I."

"Oh no, he is, you're absolutely right."

Reg Brace was looking perplexed. He could not think what Wendy had done to make the old man so docile. Or could he?

"I suppose you must get rather used to this sort of thing in your line of work," said Lady Templeton.

"You mean places like this."

"And meeting people like my husband."

"Oh no, I would say he's very special. Very different. Wouldn't you say, Reg?"

She did not even bother to follow this remark with a provoking look. Reg was so far out of his league.

"Would you very much mind if I phoned my husband?" asked Wendy.

"I would mind it very much if you didn't," Lady Templeton replied with a light laugh. "It's through in the drawing room."

She got through to Guy's office and a woman's voice answered. "Guy Howard's phone."

"Oh hello. Is he there please?"

"Oh hi, Kathy. No, he's at a meeting. He should have been back by now. Shall I tell him you called?"

"If you would. Only, you'd better tell him it's not, erm..."

"Oh hang on. Here he is now. Guy, for you."

There was a pause and Guy came on the line.

"Hello."

"Hello, Guy?"

"Yup."

"It's me."

"Er."

"Kathy."

"Oh Kathy, yes, hi. I thought you wouldn't call. How are you?"

"Not one hundred per cent myself actually."

"Oh poor you. What's the problem?"

"I think I might be Wendy."

"You what?"

"Your wife?"

"Oh. Oh, you idiot, Wembley. It's you."

"Hello."

She was now regretting that she had not maintained the pretence for just a little longer. Who knows what she might have picked up?

"So how's it gone?" asked Guy hastily. "How was he?"

"He was...very interesting."

"Didn't try and have you on the floor or anything?"

She could hear the sound of female laughter in the background. Surely Guy hadn't found out about Rourke and the Chateau Marmont. She had been very selective in her bragging. Really only the inner of inners.

"No, no," she said. "I'm all in one piece."

"Only, he's got a bit of a reputation."

"Has he?"

"I don't know. Probably. After you've finished with him."

There was more laughter in the background.

"Sorry," said Guy. "I'm under dreadful influences here. But he was good, was he?"

"I'll tell you everything when I see you. The thing is, Guy. Is Matthew still coming round tonight?"

"Yes, as far as I know. Why?"

"Because I want to see him. He is my friend too, you know."

"Right. Well, I expect he'll be here when you get back."

"Tell him if he scratches this time I'll murder him. I've got a job for him."

"What, work?"

"Yes."

"What? From Templeton?"

"Sort of."

"What a total star you are. Definitely my best deal. Matthew won't know what to say."

"Oh yes he will. He will know exactly."

"If you say so."

"I'm leaving in a few minutes, so I should be home in three hours approx."

"Well mind how you go. Wrong kind of leaves on the road and so on. Plus if you've got the painters in."

"No, Guy."

"What, bit late are they?"

"Just no, Guy."

"Fair enough."

"Hold Matthew at all costs. No slipping off to the Wanker."

"The what?"

"Blue Anchor. Think I don't know?"

"Ah."

"Honorary chap, wasn't I?"

"So you were."

"By the way, who is Kathy?"

"Kathy who?"

"Kathy me."

"Huh?"

"The one who sounds like me."

"She's... actually she's absolutely no one."

"How frightful for her."

"You what. Oh, I just heard a terrific one from Marcus. What is the Hampstead branch of Exit called?"

"Hampstead branch of Exit. I don't know."

"Ciao."

"No, don't go. Tell me."

"That's it. Ciao."

"Oh. Oh, I see."

"Must go. Call waiting. Pip pip."

"Bye."

Wendy thanked Lady Templeton again and offered the possibility of a goodbye nod to Reg Brace. He half stood as she left. If he had not been in the presence of Lady Templeton, he would have remained seated.

"And you will call us again if there's any more we can help you with."

"Yes. And likewise. You've got my number in London."

The old lady placed herself in the same spot by the front door as the car pulled out of the drive. This time her head was inclined the other way, and the right hand, instead of resting on the left, gave a little lateral wave. It was the closing section of a timeless routine.

The Vale of Evesham rolled past on either side. The first scarp of the Cotswolds sharpened to the east. Above them something strange was going on. Lear and his lines were rising into the sky like the corrugated air over a bonfire, or the ghostly surtitles of a foreign opera. She knew that she could neither stop them nor see them exactly - at least not in any conventional sense - as surely as she knew that they were there. As much as oxygen in the air, or breeze across the fields, they were there. They were as high as the shrill-gorg'd lark, they went among the crows and choughs that wing the midway air, and they twined down with rank fumiter and furrow weeds, with burdocks, hemlock, nettles, cuckoo-flowers, Darnel, and all the idle weeds that grow in our sustaining corn. Basically they were everywhere.

Wendy was not unduly alarmed, as this had happened before. It had happened all the time when she was learning Cordelia, and several times since. The thing is, it was actually quite inconvenient as it brought these immense surges of emotion at you from every side; Wagnerian storm waves sweeping from the heavens, moulten anguish rising from the bowels of the world. And so on. Take in Reuters. Blow, winds, and crack your cheeks. If it came over thundery now, that would be cheesy.

It was inconvenient because you knew it was always there, but you did not want to be disturbed by it. Like knowing that you've got Ann-Sophie Mutter or Kathleen Ferrier with you, right there on the C.D. shelves, but not playing them for months or years because of knowing they will knock you right out of true with the pain of their beauty. Shakespeare was a killer just because he was the best. He knew what you were thinking and feeling, and then he wrote it up with such brilliance that he took it all a way on from there, made you realise that what you were thinking was incomplete until he had articulated it. One of the things he knew, and knew that you knew, was the growing tawdriness of the time, the way that talentless non-entities were talked of with the same critical respect as the great; a schoolboy rapper from the West Midlands being judged as significant as Paul Robeson, a comic narrative poet on a chat show being called Chaucerian; and everyone going along with it in the sloppy delusion that the one was as valuable as the other, that low was the new high. It was a bogus inclusivity, but the sheer weight of viewing figures was bullying some quite independent minds into acceptance of the changed order. The other thing Shakespeare knew, as Wendy did, was that ambition in this altered world had turned her from an assertive, even contrary judge to an eager agent of the new equivalence.

These moments always came when she was off-guard, when something or someone nudged her involuntarily into that dangerous domain of honest self-appraisal. Today it was a scabrous old man whose farce was so far gone that it was making her weep with the tragedy of it now. Think what you would of him, he had been the conduit today... A very foolish, fond old man, fourscore and upward (just a bit) and, to deal plainly, not in his perfect mind. O! let him pass.

And his wife: her voice was ever soft, gentle and low, an excellent thing in a woman. And now here was that confounded Stratford glover's son right back in the composition of the elements, laughing through the winds at the futility of anyone, anyone writing anything while his books remained unburned. So this was his revenge for being so quotable, so usable, so handy for the adding of weight, so readily dragooned for paltry arguments and corrupt causes. Happy now, Will?

For heaven's sake, he was upsetting the spiritual monopoly of the *Bible*. It was to his words, not the apostles', that the would-be religious were turning in these difficult ragged days. For a human he was too big. Something had gone wrong. And then, just when you thought he was impossible, too high to scale, too deep to fathom, there he was, standing before you as plain as a parent.

The weight of this sad time we must obey
Speak what we feel, not what we ought to say.

You could even forgive him for going off into couplets all the time. The whoreson. Always anatomising the flaws of us, the wounded nature of humanity; always charging us, but oh so subtly, with the duty of mending, the chore of improvement.

His lines dispersed like a lapsing rainbow, and she was in the Cotswolds. The ground rose and fell, outcrops reared, the mellow stones came out and formed themselves into villages. A Liberal Democrat was on the radio telling delegates to meet the risks and face the challenges. She put Matthew's cassette on. It was too accurate for words, too true to be funny.

The light was just going as she got back to the house in Camden. Or the cottage in Primrose Hill, as Guy's tiresome mother insisted on calling it. Matthew and Guy were burning something in the kitchen. That is, it was burning and they were in another room, disabled with laughter. She could tell at a glance that they were playing Heavy Plant Crossing. This entailed doing imitations of as many people as possible, all at the same time. Matthew held the world record with nine: Tony Blair (1) saying: "I just think that things could be, well, you know, better," with Stephen Hawking's voice (2), Imran Khan's accent (3) and Tony Benn's esses (4). The figure had David Blunkett's eyes (5), Gladstone Small's neck (6), Churchill's wave (7), Naseem Hamed's left jab (8) and Max Wall's walk (9).

The contestant had to leave the room, assemble himself and then come in and walk for five paces while keeping all the other elements intact. He would go out normal and return as a wheezing mutant. It was Wendy who had named the game after a motorway sign warning motorists to look out for large construction vehicles.

Now Guy was challenging Matthew's claim to have reached ten, and Matthew was responding by shouting "Mr. Winnick's crotch" and pointing to his own. There was a great lump there which was meant to denote their priapic Latin teacher.

"No props or artifice," yelled Guy. "That's always been a rule."

"So what," said Matthew.

"So take the Jaycloth out."

"You're a hard man."

"Has to be a genuine stiffy or it doesn't count."

"OK, give us a minute then."

He was rummaging in his pants as Wendy came through the door.

"I wonder whether it's something to do with me," she said, or whether it is just one of those days."

Matthew took his hand out and looked sheepish.

"No, please carry on," she said. "You'd be in a very distinguished trend."

"What?" said Matthew.

"Hello," said Guy. "You were jolly quick."

"Yes, well don't let me disturb anything."

"You're not. We were just playing Heavy Plant Crossing, you see, and..."

"And burning the house down."

"Slight exaggeration."

She stomped through into the kitchen and turned the oven off. There was a parched stain on the floor of a saucepan, but not enough to identify what it had started out as. You'd need to get the DNA people in. The sides of the pan were translucent with heat.

Wendy sent Guy out for a take-away and sat Matthew down in the kitchen. "Jolly lucky you've been practising," she said.

"I'm always practising, haven't you noticed?"

"Did Guy tell you?"

"About the work?"

"Yes."

"He did. But I thought it must be a joke."

"And that must be your L.S.E."

"What? I went to Lamda."

"No. Low Self-Esteem."

"Don't get it."

"You're more employable than you think."

"So tell all. No, actually, wait for Guy."

When he returned with the food, she told them of her day. The studio, the voice, the obscenities, everything. At each turn their jaws fell a little further. In the disbelieving silence that followed, Matthew said with great compassion: "Oh Wendy, you can't publish that."

She was not sure whether the compassion was for her or for Sir John, and she did not ask in case she got the wrong answer. All she said was "I know, Matthew, I know." The hours grew big and the food went cold. It was after midnight when the phone went. She took the handset into the hall. It was her commissioning editor.

"Wendy? C'est moi."

"Mark."

"Sorry, but I couldn't resist it. How was he?"

"He was, he was..."

"Sorry. You must be knackered."

"No, it's fine. He was very interesting. I mean, really very interesting."

"You know there was a bit of apprehension upstairs?"

"No."

"At conference. Just that City page tosser whose name I always forget. Saying his wife had dinner with someone who said Templeton had gone dulally. You know how they're always trying to score points."

"Sure."

"But it was all right, wasn't it?"

"Oh, more than, Mark. Promise. You'll see."

"So he talked."

"He certainly did."

"About people?"

"Very much about people."

"Famous people?"

"Absolutely."

"Can you give me some quotes. Actually, sorry, I shouldn't ask now. It's very late."

He sounded like an addict trying to talk himself out of the next fix.

"I'll give you bags of quotes, Mark, I promise. Only don't let me spoil it for you by trying to remember the best ones now."

"No, no, you're right. And you are a total star."

"I'll file by Thursday morning, OK?"

"Terrific."

"How many words?"

"Let it run, from the sound of it."

"Three thousand?"

"Gosh."

"Problem?"

"No, no. Just Gosh what a lot of work. We can do a big turn from the front and hold the Hillary piece for a week."

"Hillary piece?"

"Yes. 'Mrs. President?' "

Wendy felt a nasty surge of anger that she had not been asked to write that.

"Between you and me it's not very good," he carried on.

She tried to inject a note of sympathetic disappointment into her "Oh," and felt she brought it off pretty well.

"Who's that by?" she asked breezily.

"Brenda Findlater. Between you and me it's not the greatest of pieces."

Elation. Even an involuntary punch of the air, which Guy and Matthew couldn't help noticing from the kitchen. If this meant a good mood, then good.

"I'll let you go," said Mark. "And brilliantly done."

"Thanks Mark."

"Bye."

On Thursday morning, barely ten minutes after Wendy had sent her copy through, the phone rang again. This was not a minute sooner and not a minute later than she had been expecting.

"Wendy? C'est moi."

"Mark."

He had got his champagne voice on, the one he used for effusive moments. It usually came out at bars or parties, but rarely on the phone. She prepared herself for the camp, dated vocabulary that always accompanied it.

"This is faneffingtastic. I am totallement bouleversé, stuck for words. Laughing and crying, Wendy. You are talking to one v happy camper."

"Oh Mark, thank you."

"No, no, re-foot that boot. It is just incredible. In fact, I've got two words to say to you.

"Go on."

"The first is a very little one."

"Yes?"

"And the second is slightly bigger."

"Let's take the first one first."

"Al."

"And the second?"

"Italian."

"That's an airline, isn't it. You're not going to send me to interview an airline."

"No, no. Pacino. Al Pacino."

There was a pause.

"Scarface," Mark followed up.

"Yes, yes, I know who Al Pacino is."

"He's yours."

"That's…" Now Wendy tried to find the right balance between "That's unbelievable" and "I can probably fit that in." Again, she felt she got it about right.

"Blanche Hettner's been on and said yes."

"Goodness. But wouldn't that be one for, you know…"

"Brenda?"

"Yes. I'd have thought…" An initiative of sisterly support came out stillborn.

"So would Sir John Templeton be one for Brenda. Except that Brenda could never get him talking like that. It's incredible. And did he actually volunteer all that stuff about the affair with the woman who died?"

"Well, I wouldn't say volunteered," said Wendy. "But, well, you know." She did her best to sound modest.

"It's so moving," said Mark. "So tragic."

"Thank you, Mark." It struck her what a strange thing it was to draw such praise for the revelation of private sadness, but then kicked the thought out at once.

"And the baby and everything," he went on.

"It is dreadful, isn't it."

"And you know, one of the things it made me think when I was reading it was how incredibly much everything has changed since then. I mean, can you imagine some bloke threatening to smash a woman's career if she refused to get rid of his baby?"

Wendy found she could imagine it all too easily, but did not think it would be wise to say so. Instead she said "I'm really glad you like it, Mark."

"And he's never said all this stuff before, has he?"

"Definitely not. We're the first."

"And all the quotes on Olivier and Burton and Taylor etc. People will love that."

"I hope so."

"The other thing is, Wendy, it's so well written. The house and everything. You've got him to a tee. I can just hear him in my head. I think probably the only thing we're going to have to tone down, just a little, will be the physical description of him. The clothes and that."

"Sure."

"I'm not saying it's not accurate, just that you know how they can be upstairs."

"No, I know."

"But anyway I'm thrilled. It'll be in on the twelfth. Why don't you come in the week before, when we're laying out. You could help us with the pictures. We don't see enough of you anyway."

"I'd love to."

"Thursday?"

"That's fine."

"See you then."

"Bye."

When she arrived at the office it was noon, early enough not to look as though she was wanting to be taken out to lunch and feted, but late enough to go along with the idea if it came up. She moved confidently down the open plan of the weekend section. The flow of people that went along its length would sometimes sweep loudly on into the design room, sometimes peel off in eddies among the small flanking rooms and whisper. On the half-floor above them she could see smart young men with earnest faces. From the columns they wrote you might have expected them to be donnish old figures who had caught the end of national service. They could not be accused of too much liberalism, and yet there was a tweedy, avuncular quality to their prose. In fact, these men were pink-faced and chubby, courting the bagginess of middle age long before it fell naturally due. One or two of them were closet Portillistas who since the rout were not entirely certain as to how or what they should be.

Away to the right of her she saw a group of people around the light-box. One of them, the tallest, was Desmond Hale, the head of the section. He was looking, she had to admit, really very acceptable. He was not long divorced and was just entering a self-confident phase. It showed in his short new hair and in the Paul Smith suit which he would never have worn when he was married.

There were about eight people in the group and they seemed to be drinking wine. Brenda Findlater was there, looking gratifyingly sour and glancing at her watch. This was a moment of triumph. Desmond Hale was the first to see Wendy arriving.

"That's a wonderful piece," he said, and then blushed fetchingly when there was laughter at the double-entendre. "I'll start again. It's a wonderful article, Wendy. I don't know how you managed. None of us do."

Brenda Findlater made one last play for attention by saying how maligned Paraguay had been by the international community.

"There was no torture at all when I was there," she said, but no one was listening. She thought about making a polite suggestion of other questions that Wendy might have asked Sir John, giving her the benefit of her own great experience, but there really wasn't an audience for it. She put her glass down, hung her face and scurried off like a dung beetle. It was not possible to have more than one person being good at old people.

On the light-box were sundry photos of Sir John, going back and back through the roles and periods with which she had become so familiar. She felt the smell of the house and the autumn hills, and the sound of that old voice coming up from a buried place. Next to the photos was a rough proof of her article, with quotes picked out from the text in big type: "When I think of how I behaved towards that poor girl, I feel more remorse than Othello, more blood on my hands than Macbeth."

"Pleased?" said Mark.

"It looks wonderful," she replied.

"Hard to believe, some of it," said Desmond Hale.

"Is it?" Immediately these words were out, she knew she had sounded more alarmed than she had meant to.

"Yes. Given what we know of the old boy. Or, what we thought we knew."

"Yes, of course," said Wendy.

"Still," Desmond Hale continued. "All on tape I expect."

"Absolutely," said Wendy

But could they really be drinking wine to celebrate her article? They could not. Beyond the proofs, on a desk, was a little pile of books; half a dozen copies of the same one. Standing next to them, shy as a shadow, was their author. It was Melanie Woolf, the young sub-editor who had befriended Wendy.

"We're giving Melanie a sort of little extra office launch for her book," explained Desmond Hale.

"Ah," said Wendy. She felt something being pierced inside her. It was too soon to know what damage was being done, but it was obviously grave.

"People think we're tight-fisted here, but compared to publishers we are rank amateurs in the art of meanness."

"Yes," said Wendy blankly.

"It's a terrific achievement," said Hale. "And a publisher like that."

Wendy let her eye pass down the spine of a copy. The eye brought back evidence of a distressingly famous and successful imprint. Desmond handed her a copy. It was called The Tarnished Muse. According to the blurb it was a mischievous comedy of media mores, with an unsparing eye for the vanities of its twinkling stars.

"I expect we're all in it," said Mark, rather hoping that he was.

No roman a clef, swore the blurb, this was ultimately a hard-hitting and timely essay on the public ownership of private lives.

Whatever had been pierced was now haemorrhaging. It was even more serious than Wendy had feared. And there was worse to come. It was waiting in the opening pages. Melanie Woolf's anti-heroine had a double-barrelled name of spurious origin - Wendy's mind refused to absorb the name itself - and always let it be known, soon after meeting someone, that she had played Ophelia at Christchurch and sung in the Bach Choir.

The cow. The totalfuckingcow. She couldn't do that. She was recycling Wendy for so-called fictive purposes, and doing it so that everyone would know. And the trade journals were already calling her things like wise and important. Sod the routine disclaimer about the characters in this book bearing no relation to any living persons. That's what everyone put in when they knew that everyone would know what they were up to. And so true to life, said the blurb, that everybody in this sad and seductive world would find themselves looking into the mirror with fresh eyes.

That last sentence was the blade twisted in the wound. It removed even the consolation of being the model of the lampoon. Melanie Woolf's satire was so inclusive that no one was safe. And in that way she camouflaged her public offence while declaring herself very clearly to her private quarry. So this is why she had been so friendly, so butter-wouldn't-melt, all this time. And then going back to her flat in the evening, her horrible, single, functional, survivor flat in Tulse Hill or whatever unthinkable south London place it was, and working her, Wendy, into a timely, much-needed, hard-hitting...no, no, it was too much to think about. That way madness lay. Soon there would be author-interviews (who would do them?) in which Melanie Woolf would say how she had honed her writing skills by ironing the bumps from supposedly professional prose; how she had made a list of other writers' errors and resolved to avoid them herself.

One of the other sub-editors, a plump middle-aged man with a kind, librarian face, had already read it in uncut proof, and said it was "brilliant and very fair, particularly the come-uppance."

Come-uppance. With the resolution of a suicide, Wendy leafed through a few of the late pages. The double-barrelled anti-heroine was to be found slumped in a north London graveyard, "her once keen and sought-after face made bruised and blotchy by her own and others' hands."

She took a gulp of wine and heard her own voice say something. The words sounded as though they were coming from someone else. "I say, Melanie," she said. "Many congratulations. What a dark horse you are."

Back home in Camden she stomped about the house, crying and shouting and wanting a baby. The phone rang. She heard her own voice saying "oh hello" at the other end before the line went dead. She must be losing it a little.

Guy came home with Matthew and said "Hello Wembley." Seeing that she was in "a bit of a black one," the two of them went off and played Heavy Plant Crossing while she went up to bed and sobbed. In the sanctuary of approaching sleep she lay deep and unseen, crown'd with rank fumiter and furrow weeds, with burdocks, hemlock, nettles, cuckoo flowers, darnel, and all the idle weeds...

Things looked up. The Templeton piece hit the streets. It caused at least the mild sensation that had been hoped for, and she was consoled by the thought that her readers outnumbered Melanie Woolf's by several hundred to one. Better still, *The Tarnished Muse* got a crumpling notice in the *Literary Review*. She was aware of some raves knocking about, but managed to avoid them. *The Review* dismissed it as "the preenings of a twelfth-rate wit trading on the name of a famous family." Wendy felt a personal debt of gratitude towards the reviewer, a woman called Margot Isherwood. The other heartening discovery was that by not actually reading *The Tarnished Muse*, she deprived it of its power.

Other people might have been doing the same to her, but many were not. The phone rang incessantly through the weekend and well into the following week. There were calls from old friends who always knew she was going to do something special; calls from umpteen papers asking if she would consider a similar article on

Sir Royston Lushington, who she thought had been dead for ten years; calls from Mark at the office saying "Two words. The first is Clint." And finally a call from Desmond Hale no less, asking her for, well, basically, when it came down to it, a date.

"It's just that I've got a spare ticket for the Ian Holm Lear at the National. And I really couldn't think of anyone more appropriate."

"And so you tried me."

"Yes. Oh dear, does that sound awful?"

"No, no. I'll have to check..."

"Of course."

"No."

"If there's a problem."

"No, I think I'd love to come."

"And I thought maybe we could have a chat about work."

"Oh dear."

"No, quite the reverse."

"I'd love to come. Actually."

They met, nervously, in the mouth of the Cottesloe. He looked anxious and bashful, like teenage boys used to when they had at last found the courage to ask her out.

He did say "I'm so glad it's you I'm seeing this with. I feel sort of safe. I'm dreadfully ignorant you know."

She tried to say something about it not being important to know things, but it didn't quite work out. The lights went down and the mighty machinery of the play started up, driven unstoppably round by its great pentameter motor. It forged the elemental words and embossed them on the air. Shakespeare, it went without saying, was doing it again. Now, as never before, the lines had her name on them. This time different lines than usual. Surprising lines. Have more than thou owest, speak less than thou showest. Into her womb convey sterility. Thou whoreson Zed! thou unnecessary letter. That sir which serves and seeks for gain And follows but for form Will pack when it begins to rain And leave thee in the storm. O!, sir! you are old;

Nature in you stands on the very verge of her confine. I will have such revenges on you both. A poor infirm weak and despis'd old man. I am not in my perfect mind. The weight of this sad time we must obey, Speak what we feel not what we ought to say. The oldest hath borne most: we that are young Shall never see so much nor live so long.

Afterwards, in the silence that always follows, Desmond Hale asked the familiar question - why Cordelia has to die. "I mean, I'm sure he knew what he was doing. But well, what was he doing?"

They were sitting in the Archduke, under the line out of Charing Cross.

"Yes, it's a tricky one, isn't it," she said, and was silent. She was thinking, of course, about her father, and wishing it could all have been different. As daughters do, at the end of such a play. Fathers too.

"Well, not now maybe," said Hale. "It's not going to go away, is it?"

"Hardly."

"It's quite late. Shall we order?"

As they ate she noticed a look coming into his face that she used to see in boys when they were going to ask her if they could kiss her. Instead he asked if he could see her again, and she felt her head nodding yes. Surely he must know she was married. Technically. But then, if Guy wasn't acting as if he was, why should she?

She took a taxi back to Camden. When she got home she found a note from Guy saying he was round at Matthew's and would see her later. The following morning she woke up in an empty bed. To her surprise she found that instead of being worried by his absence, it was taking the edge off her prospective guilt.

There were two phone calls within half an hour. Both were from old women with the good manners to have delayed their calls until they knew she would be less busy. The first was from Aunt Beatrice,

"It's me dear. Is this a bad moment?"

"No, it's fine."

"Just to say how fascinating I found your article on Johnny Templeton. As you can imagine, I could hardly believe my eyes."

"Yes, wasn't it extraordinary?"

"Just after we had been talking about it."

"I know. I was going to be in touch, but I guessed you'd probably seen it anyway."

"Oh, I wouldn't have missed it for anything, dear. And he just sort of volunteered it, did he?"

"Yes."

"Well, I never. It must have been building up in him all those years. But I say, clever you for getting it all out of him. You know, my heart almost softened towards him. I say, almost. But what about his poor wife, eh? It's chaps, isn't it. They don't make it easy on a girl."

Yes, what about Lady T.? Wendy had rather put her out of her mind, just as she had done with Melanie Woolf's book.

The question did not remain untended for long. When the phone went again it was an even older, and lighter voice.

"Mrs. Howard-Watt?"

"Speaking."

"Oh hello, it's Clarissa Templeton here."

"Hello."

"I do hope this is not a bad moment."

"No, not at all."

"Good. Well, I read the article."

"Ah," said Wendy. "I rather feared you might."

"Oh dear. Shouldn't I have?"

"No, no, not at all. I mean, I don't mean that."

Wendy was not sure what she meant, except perhaps that she was sorry. She knew that she was going to have the greatest difficulty putting these feelings into words for Sir John's wife. Lady Templeton must have sensed her unease, and moved into her diplomatic manner.

"It was jolly nice to have you here the other day."

"It was jolly nice of you to have me."

"And you'll drop by again if you're up this way, won't you. We'd be delighted to see you. It's divine here at the moment, as you can imagine."

"It must be lovely."

"Quite our favourite time."

Was that it? Just a call to say she'd read it, as her code of conduct required. That and the routine invitation of the upper mids, which no one expects to be followed up. Nothing more? No comment? No outrage, alarm, lawyers?

"Mine too," said Wendy.

There was a royal yes, and a pause. Then Lady Templeton said: "Now, let me see. Who was it who said tell the truth and shame the devil?"

"Probably Shakespeare," said Wendy.

"Yes, it generally is, isn't it."

"I think it's *Henry IV, Part One*."

"That would tally, certainly. Well, anyway, it's rather what you've done, isn't it?"

"Oh?"

"Yes. I mean to say, there it is."

"I see," said Wendy. She didn't.

"Although he does come across as a bit of a devil himself, doesn't he, but I'm sure we can let that pass."

"Look," said Wendy with a sudden rush of candour, or fear. "If what I wrote caused you offence, I'm most dreadfully sorry."

"No, no, Mrs. Howard-Watt. With respect I think you are misunderstanding me. You told the truth, both of you. Who said truth will come to light? I don't think we need answer that. 'Truth will come to light. Murder cannot be hid long.' "

The last words were more declaimed than spoken.

"Anyway," she went on, "you are both to be commended for it."

Wendy did not think sarcasm was one of Lady Templeton's modes, and she was right.

"I am only sorry," the voice continued, "if he was a little, how shall we say, curmudgeonly with you."

"Oh no, really," said Wendy. "It was fine."

"You see, between you and me, he is perfectly agreeable to those he knows, but apparently he has started being a touch unpredictable with strangers. I would have come in with you myself, but he never seems to talk freely when I do. So it's as well I stayed out."

"Yes, I'm sure it is," said Wendy.

She was burning to know if Sir John had seen the piece, but dared not ask.

"I was particularly interested in your article," said Lady Templeton, "because so often they don't tell you anything interesting at all. As you yourself must know."

"Absolutely."

"And over the years I have always been grateful to the ones that have helped me to glean a little more information."

"About anything in particular?"

"I mean about my husband. And yours, I have to say, was quite the most informative."

"You really don't have to thank me, Lady Templeton."

"Well, I'm not sure that I am, exactly." There was another light laugh at the end of the phone. "But you know, I had always rather wondered what was going on during that *Winter's Tale* tour. There was something very strange. He didn't want me anywhere near it. And now it's all fallen into place. It was young Kitty Collingham. The poor girl. And a good actress. You'll not have seen a photograph of her here, or of that production, and you probably don't need me to explain why."

Wendy thought she could hear a slight shake in the impeccable voice. But it carried on. Perhaps Wendy really was as good a listener as they said she was. "I had said that I would play if needed, d'you see. Not Hermione, of course, but perhaps Paulina. But John wouldn't have his wife going out to work. Not when he was providing quite well for both of us. And for that I suppose I should be grateful. Our friends have always been rather tickled by the fact that I should have stopped being a Knight to then become a Lady.

Clarissa Knight, you see. Not that that would mean anything to anybody."

Wendy felt a wave of anger and compassion. She wanted to hug the tiny, noble bird-body that had never been able to supply the conditions for procreation. She found herself mourning, deep and bitter, the barren decades of the mid-century when Clarissa Knight might have exercised her own equal right to a gloriously mounting career. Clarissa Knight as Viola in the legendary *Twelfth Night* at Stratford; Clarissa Knight as the apotheosis of pre-war Cleopatras; as a redefining Portia, an enigmatic Gertrude, a Lady M. of frightening power. None had come to pass. Not one. Not a photo, review, programme or handbill to hint at the possibility of such an appearance. Not a murmur in the memories of old buffs, not an echo in the refurbished Gods of the ancient reps. She was a boat that might have sailed at full billow but for the single sharp rock of no wife of John's going out to work.

Wendy would have like to ask her whether there was anything she regretted about the arrangement. But as she was not interviewing her she felt she lacked the licence. Instead, she finally asked the question which she had privately wanted to ask ever since the article appeared: had Sir John read the thing? And what on earth had he said about it?

It came out a little more elliptically than that. "I do hope your husband wasn't too much put out, didn't mind too much."

"By what?"

"By anything I said."

"Well, it wasn't you saying it, was it?"

"I beg your pardon."

"It was him. He could hardly have been put out by something he said himself, now could he?"

Had Lady Templeton seen through her? Wendy felt a dart of panic at her own carelessness. She would have to watch her words. That was her profession.

"As a matter of fact," Lady Templeton went on, "I'm afraid he was quite indifferent to it."

"Oh."

It could have been worse.

"Yes, quite indifferent. But that is, one might say, another story. Really another story."

"I see," said Wendy.

"No, with respect, I don't think you do see. And now I really must let you get on, Mrs. Howard-Watt. I've taken up quite enough of your time already, and I do know how busy you are."

"Lady T..."

"Goodbye now."

She hung up. By coincidence, above the town of Malvern, Sir John Templeton had at that very moment made his way down the imposing staircase and turned right into the drawing room to find his wife finishing a phone call. In the language by which they understood each other he asked her who she was speaking to, and she replied that it was the young woman who had been down to see him a few weeks ago. He nodded and smiled.

"Yes, it was a nice article, John, wasn't it."

He nodded again.

"Shall I read it to you once more. Just once?"

Another nod.

They sat down beside the fire and she took up the paper that he was now far too long-sighted to see properly. She began reading: "On a perfect autumn day in his beautiful Malvern home, Sir John Templeton, our most distinguished knight of the stage, looked back on three score and ten years of professional glory and marital happiness."

He shifted in his seat and gave a deep, resonant purr. "Yes, it is rather good, I must confess. Do go on."

"He showed me cherished photographs of his legendary performances in the major roles, playing opposite the greatest actresses of the century. And he shared with me the secrets of his unbroken love for the remarkable woman who has been with him from the beginning."

And so on and so on, until Sir John's nods were not of approval but of encroaching sleep and he dozed off on the pillow of eternal approbation. If the words were a little familiar to him, and if he thought that he had heard them several times before, he was not letting on. Besides, these people in the papers, they did repeat each other so.

And if Lady Templeton grew weary of reading the same text over and over again, she was not letting on either. She might vary it a little next time. After all, it was a composite, pulled together from many different publications over many years. It was not badly done, though she said so herself. And whatever its shortcomings it was right in line with the demands of the readership. That, surely, was the main thing.

About a month later Wendy was having dinner with Desmond Hale at the Etoile in Charlotte Street. "You know, Wendy," he said, "in a couple of years we're really going to have to do a book of your interviews. You wait and see. Once we've got a few monsters in the bag. A few Minellis and Streisands or whoever they are these days. You're much better informed there than I am."

"Sheryl Crow," said Wendy.

"Yes, her. Very good. And then perhaps even Mandela? Bush? Both Bushes? There's going to be a time."

Wendy Howard-Watt gets to the heart of George Senior and his Outer Child.

"By the way," he continued, "we're ninety per cent there with Tom Jones. If that's OK."

"Sure."

"He wants to do it at the Chateau Marmont. Apparently he's got a favourite room there."

"That's fine. Really."

"Didn't you do something there once before?"

She was aware of her face start to pinken and glisten. Joey Rourke breaking off the interview with a genial "Aw Hell," standing up and then sort of diving through the air onto her where she sat, roughing her up a little, carrying her over his shoulder into the bedroom. Dumping her on the bed and then the waft of a cowboy leather smell as he took his boots off and started to reveal his ten-million-dollar-a-movie (probably twice that now) physique.

"Are you OK, Wendy?" said Desmond.

" Fine. Great."

These last words couldn't have been truer; she may have made a mental jump-cut to 8221 Sunset Boulevard, West Hollywood, but the man who was with her there was not the actor who had made his name with *Streets of Meat*, but the man in charge of the entire weekend operation of Britain's most popular serious newspaper, Desmond Hale.

"You do keep your tapes, don't you?" he asked.

The question threw her. She answered "Oh yes," then hurriedly tacked on some room for manoeuvre with "I think so." Why did he want to know? Had there been a complaint about inaccuracy? Some inquiry from the theatre world perhaps? Or from the Worcester area?

He saw her anxiety and said quickly: "For the book, that's all. In case they want you to expand some of the pieces."

"Yes. Of course. I've got them all."

Some confidence had come into his manner. He paid the bill and they left. As a taxi drew up and they said goodbye on the pavement, he mentioned the Paris idea again and she promised she would tell him by the weekend. He was optimistic about her answer.

When she got home she went into her study to check her phone messages. There were her tapes, her growing number of famous scalps, fanning out nicely at the back of the desk. As she looked at them now it was with an even more proprietorial eye than before. Quite soon, next year if her hit-rate continued, they would all be living cosily together in a little hard cover home with her own name on the front. And the side. All their lives, with their respective triumphs and tragedies, highs and heartaches, would coalesce in the identity of the author who had been there for them all when they (or at least their PR consultants) had needed her. And she, no less than Melanie Woolf – actually a lot more than swotty little library-skinned closet prose stylist Melanie Woolf – would be important and wise and all those other knackered epithets that got showered on anyone who'd ever written a Size Zero slimmy on their Polish Au Pair Year.

Here was Mary Archer (not fragrant at all, should have been tougher with her, particularly about choice of husband); Sting (world's vainest man, no contest, kept sitting himself near mirrors - shouldn't have used the phrase effortless masculinity); Anita Roddick (should have pressed her about her dodgy Amazon Indian friends); Joan Collins (how long did that face really take?); and so on: Joanna Lumley (surprisingly bad-tempered), Geoffrey Archer ("an example to us all"), Kate Moss, (too stoned to speak – all quotes worked up from cuttings), Jackie Mason (truly funny),

Mary and Geoffrey Archer (must try to forget that one), Joan Collins again, then the assorted lesser ones of slightly before: a profoundly deaf stand-up ("I never hear the boos"), a man of one hundred and ten ("Can you speak up, love?"); a Bradford shop girl who woke up one morning to find she could only speak Lithuanian. And, as they say in press releases, many more, not forgetting the most recent triumph, Sir John Templeton ("A masterpiece" – chief sub-editor, weekend section.) But where was he? The old boy was hiding. She rummaged in the desk drawers, in her handbag, in her cassette recorder, checked on all the other shelves and surfaces, but the peerless thespian had done the vanishing trick.

Downstairs in the drawing room Matthew and Guy were watching European football. They had just been to a party given by one of Matthew's friends. Guy was morose with drink. Perhaps something other than drink as well. When Wendy came in he barely looked up. Locatelli picked this moment to drive in a thirty-yard equaliser for Fiorentina, but even this caused only a flicker of interest.

"Hello Wendy," said Matthew.

"Hello boys."

"Good evening then?"

"Yes, OK," said Wendy. "Just some people from the office. So a bit shop really."

"Actually we bumped into some of your office pals at the party."

"Oh really." The news was more frightening than interesting.

"A little group of them," said Matthew. "Novelist woman. Mousy. Can't remember her name. And the one you don't like. Brenda."

"Goodness, what were they doing there?"

"Friends of friends I think."

"Yes. Well. I don't suppose either of you have seen a tape about?"

"What tape?" asked Matthew.

"My cassette of Sir John. The one we did."

"Search me I'm afraid."

"Guy."

No response.

"Oh, well," said Wendy, I expect he'll turn up. It's just that... never mind. I'm going to bed. I'm knackered."

The following morning, an hour after Guy had gone to work, silent and suffering, the phone rang.

"Wendy?"

"Yes?"

"It's me."

"Oh Desmond hi. Thanks so much for..."

"No, not Desmond actually."

"Matthew."

How could he do people he hadn't even met? It was uncanny.

"Morning."

"Do you ever use your own voice?" She sounded angry.

"D'you mind if I come round?"

"What, now?"

"Yes."

He sounded different. Urgent. The impression was confirmed by his appearance. They stood in the kitchen without saying anything. There was a strange new disapproval on him. The muscles which normally served to pull his face into wonderful mutations were taut and serious and very much in his control. Wendy was aware of looking shifty and tried to temper it with defiance.

"Go on then," she said.

"You were asking after Sir John Templeton last night."

"Yes. You know where he is?"

"He has returned to the arms of his creator."

"Do you mean he's dead? Is it on the radio? Goodness, I was the last, then."

"I mean that I have taken back the tape."

"Oh, thank goodness it's safe."

"Is it?"

"What are you getting to, Matthew? What's going on?"

"Is anyone safe?"

"I don't understand. Matthew. Please just say what you mean."

"Who is Desmond Hale?"

Her face went hot.

"He is a bloke at work. He runs the section. Why?"

"I'm interested. And Guy's interested."

"Frankly Matthew, I'm amazed to hear Guy's interested in anything except you."

"Oh come on, Wendy."

"Or possibly Kathy. I'm rather confused, to be honest. Who is Kathy anyway?"

"No one as far as I know. I mean, no one special. Just someone he knows."

"Knows how?"

"Through work, I suppose. You know how he's always, well, getting to know people. Or sort of know them."

Wendy said nothing, but made a face which suggested to Matthew that she didn't know whether to find his honest explanation satisfactory. He took advantage of the silence and said sharply: "Who is Desmond Hale?"

She was surprised by his tone and replied: "I've told you, Matthew." It was defensive, but with a little curve of outrage thrown in at the last minute.

"Told me, yes. But not really told me. Hey?"

She walked in a small circle and returned to where she was standing, at the corner of the table. She was aware of being studied with a closeness that no one else could match. It must account for his sublime powers of reproduction - and for his danger. He could see inside, damn him, when most people were quite happy to accept the top layer. She wondered if it might be best to let him into the Desmond Hale business, buy him off with a small confidence. She didn't wonder long; if he got a sniff of the truth, he would not rest until he had extracted everything from her. That was another thing he did better than anyone else. He really should have been far more successful than he was. Then he would have better things to do than hang around in the lives and the marriages of his old friends.

She decided to say, very firmly: "Actually Matthew, and with respect. It's none of your business."

"I'm afraid I do consider Guy my business. I'm sorry, but there it is."

"Are you still in love with him? Is that how it is?"

"Not like that, no. Not for years. As you know very well. Or should do. As his wife. But do I love him? Yes, I do. And that's why I'm doing what I'm doing. No other reason."

"And what are you doing, Matthew?"

He was pleased with himself. Delighted actually, and saw no merit in hiding it. "Well, I suppose you could say I've got the old boy hostage. He's quite safe and I am treating him with all the respect he deserves. And I also suppose one could say that he's sort of got you hostage as well. I must say, it is funny how it goes."

"Matthew, you wouldn't," said Wendy. All the urgency had passed to her.

"My witness of course is your husband, who is hardly likely to land his own wife in the shit. Unless he is sorely provoked. That's what we've both liked about Guy, isn't it. And always have. His natural sense of laissez-faire."

There was another piercing of something vital inside her, the same grievous rip she had experienced over Melanie Woolf. She wondered how many of these she could sustain without going under; how many compartments had to be flooded for the boat of her to sink. How she regretted the alliance she had fallen into with him, early on, because of their shared affection for Guy. She should have known then it was a double-edged accommodation, the kind that causes terrible carnage on disintegration. He was standing at the far end of the kitchen, sticking close to the door in case she flew at him. He had seen Guy's bruises in the past and didn't fancy his own chances in single combat with her. He was up for a health bar advert and didn't want to go in with visible damage.

"Matthew," she said eventually, "you are, at the end of the day, a vicious, vengeful, waspish old queen."

He weighed the adjectives carefully and, like Wendy, assessed the damage. This was above the waterline. He had been called far worse than that. In fact he looked quite pleased to have had so much thought and so many adjectives lavished on him.

"That's all fair enough, Wendy," he said. "Except for the old. That doesn't happen for another fifteen years. At least, not to some of us." Somehow he managed to inflect the last sentence in a way that caused her new and quite unexpected levels of pain. She could feel her jaw dragged to one side with the flinch of it. She knew that if she straightened herself again and looked back at him she would see a hood-eyed and reptilian figure, smirking like a gorged snake.

"And you've missed out gifted. Gifted I would really have appreciated."

Wendy had never believed in the idea of people tearing their hair. It seemed so pointless, so guaranteed to add yet another layer of grief and trouble to what you already had. You'd have to put the hair back, which would be impossible. Or you'd have to apply plaster to the ravaged scalp, which would also be impracticable. So you'd have to end up shaving your head, which would mean you wouldn't have any hair to speak of for a long time. But now; now she found herself re-thinking her position. A few good hanks of hair snatched out of the top of her with the sound of ripping vegetation. It was making a strange kind of sense. A really good piece of self-deracination. But then a blizzard arrived in her head and she could not see out of it.

Matthew was talking again. "Of course, Wendy, what is definitely not my business is your business. I mean your work. I'm a stranger there and frankly, in a way, thank God. So things like contacts, who you know, what one does with one's material once one has got it - all these things are a bit of a mystery to me. Although I am a tad less ignorant after last night."

"Last night."

"At my friend's party. Melanie Thingy. Famous. From your work. Woolf. And that nice cuddly Brenda woman. Her I like. Very, what's the word, approachable. He's obviously nice, too."

"Who?" She shouldn't have asked, but she did, and now it was too late to un-ask.

"Him," said Matthew, flat as he could get it.

"No, Matthew, you're not going to."

"They all said very nice things about him. How nice to work for and that. Not going to what?"

"You know perfectly well. You're not going to tell them about the tape. Our tape."

"You say our tape."

"Oh, yours then. You know what I mean."

" Except it was your idea. Credit where it's due, I say."

" You wouldn't though, would you."

" Do what?"

"Tell them."

"I should hope not. I mean, you wouldn't go round suggesting things to someone who you didn't think you could trust, now would you?"

"It would be," said Wendy, not following Matthew's shift from the particular to the general, "I mean, it really would be well and truly out of order, don't you think."

"On that," said Matthew plainly and directly, "we are in agreement."

What next? Had Desmond Hale also put in an appearance at this party, after saying goodnight to her? Unlikely, but not impossible. And had Matthew spoken to him there, been charming to him and somehow found out about his interest in Wendy? His more than interest. Or had he just plugged into the gossip about her and Desmond that would have been circulating there?

The two stood in silence, looking at each other but also not looking. Nothing was coming from Matthew. Nor was it about to. No initiatives, no climb-downs, no compromises. He knew what he knew, and had passed to her the responsibility for what he might or might not do with that knowledge. It was outrageous. So perverse, so ungrateful, so literally queer. It was probably he who had made Guy the way he was. Whatever way that was. Why did this man have to be in their lives so endlessly and utterly?

She was about to say something – she had no idea what - when there was the sound of the key in the front door. It could only be Guy. There were no other candidates. Wendy and Matthew found themselves looking up involuntarily at each other, as if posing the inevitable questions: what was Guy doing here? What was Guy going to think the two of them were doing here? What were they going to tell Guy they were doing here? Before they could move forward to the discussion stage, Guy was in the house, passing the open kitchen door. He did notice them as he went by, but only just, and muttered "Oh hello you two." It was an entirely dead delivery, without surprise, pleasure, anxiety or anger. Certainly without judgement. Guy never did judgement. It was without anything really. Perhaps something dreadful had happened at work. The financial climate had suddenly turned foul, as it kept threatening to, and Guy had to be let go.

They heard his feet dragging him sadly upstairs. Then there was a sudden increase in the pace, and a growling noise. It sounded like a wild animal being reined back by force, but was in fact just the beginning of a major vomit - what Guy and Matthew would call Epic Chunder. As he hadn't found the time or strength to close the lavatory door behind him, everything was audible: the next strangulated heave - the animal pushing out of the tunnel now - and the first noise, between spill and scatter, on the Amtico tiling. Guy might have been trying to say something, a simple notion like Christ or Shit, but the next wave was launching up from his floor, and the words were forced into a single expletive made entirely of vowels.

Matthew and Wendy had been listening with their faces dipped. This could have been out of respect for the suffering of a close one, but was more likely out of embarrassment. When they did look up again, they saw their own mix of feelings in each other's eyes. There was sympathy and concern, yes, but there was also the glint of suppressed hilarity. Their coalition might have fractured, but they still had the common ground on which it had been founded - Guy. He could now be heard making the sounds of slow recovery: serious regular breathing, then a low, chastened groan.

"Must have been something he ate," said Wendy.

"Yes," said Matthew. "Or else anxiety."

Wendy was on the brink of saying "anxiety about what?", but pulled back just in time. It was just what Matthew would have wanted her to ask. Then he could pull one of his arch, you-tell-me faces. Instead, she said "Or both."

"Yes," said Matthew. "Or both."

Now the sounds from upstairs were of a half-hearted mopping-up operation. Paper was being slid across surfaces and stuffed into the toilet. The flush was struggling with the load and making one of its muffled cries for help. The water was welling perilously close to the lip and Guy was trying to fight down a potential flood with the brush. In the kitchen Wendy and Matthew were laughing openly. Inwardly, she was wishing that Guy would grow up, while Matthew was regretting he had grown up to the extent that he had. They could hear him leave the toilet and pad delicately into the bedroom. The bedsprings gave one of the metallic whimpering noises that had so amused him - and Wendy too - in the early days. They had once even tried to synchronise their own sounds with it.

"We ought to see if he's OK," said Matthew.

"Yes," said Wendy. "We ought."

They could both have left the kitchen and gone up the stairs together, but they didn't. They were making rather polite, deferential gestures at each other, as if to say "Do you want to do it?" Eventually it was Wendy who went, and Matthew who stayed. She went with complicated feelings. Complicated feelings were becoming the rule rather than the exception. Not for the first time she was surprised to find compassion and resentment living in her, side by side. And then of course there was disappointment. This was less surprising, because disappointment always stalked everything, biding its time for an opening. Often it was the disappointment of opportunities perishing before they had been given a proper chance. Once again she thought of Little Lady Templeton and her brave face of a life. And once again she put the thought from her head as fast as she decently could. She had herself to think of. Guy's voice was coming from the bedroom. It was softer and more vulnerable than she had heard it for a long time. He was saying "So sorry about this." It did sound like a very committed apology, she had to admit. A big one too, as if there was plenty of it to go around and cover other areas. She also wondered if she might be hearing a previously undetected element; like someone who has heard the same piece of music for years but then discovers a fresh harmonic strand in the mix. She thought she might even be hearing the sound of contrition. Then she wondered if she was only hearing it because she had no choice, but quickly put the question aside for another day. Contrition was not the easiest emotion to find, her father used to say: but value it, Wendy, value it, because it promises change as surely as the cuckoo promises spring. She'd been all of eight when he'd handed down this and other slabby heirlooms of advice, and it had never occurred to her that they might be of any use. Like an old valve radio that still gets a clear signal.

Downstairs in the kitchen Matthew gathered his jacket from the chair back and went into the hall. He stood for a second at the foot of the stairs and thought about calling up to say he was off. Instead he let himself out through the front door and closed it behind him as quietly as he could. He was practised in the ways of the latch. Down the road and round the corner, half way back to his flat, he started thinking about his own behaviour. Snatches of an old conversation came into his head; a conversation with Guy, perhaps. No, Wendy. It was with Wendy, and it was about Shakespeare. He remembered phrases: the duty of mending, the chore of improvement. That sort of thing; big, humourless, carbolic phrases that spoke of the need to raise your game, to be better than you had been previously. He was still a relative stranger to such self-negotiation. He tended to just behave, often badly, and not think about it. This time however, he found himself looking at the possibility that he had placed himself squarely on the side of morality and altruism. If it was true, it would take some getting used to. He would get safely to bed, that was the first thing, and then hope to wake up in the morning feeling good about his conduct, his motivation and all those difficult related things. He felt he deserved to, just as a good diplomat deserves his share of the peace dividend. Meanwhile, safely out of sight, he allowed the slight disappointment to come up and take possession of his usually clever and dissembling features. This time there was nothing he could do to alter his face. It was going the way it wanted to go, and was not bothered about what he thought. At least no one was watching.

THE NIGHT EVERY-THING HAPPE-NED

I'll start by admitting that I never liked my grandmother. I'll go further and say I hated her and everything she stood for. I kept it to myself because to have said this in our family would have been like slagging off the monarchy to a bunch of high Tories. You only do it if you want trouble, and I already had plenty of my own to be going on with. I privately hoped she would die before too long so that the rest of us - my mother, my sister and me - could start to be honest about her. She lived just round the corner from us in one of the original mansion blocks, and her presence in our lives was like a huge central falsehood from which any number of smaller lies drew their life. But what I want to say is that these feelings of mine had nothing at all to do with the message that was left on her answering machine that day. I would go to the stake on that. But so what, I reckon I'm going there anyway now.

What happened was this. My girlfriend Alice had just moved into one of the mews cottages nearby. Her phone number was virtually the same as my grandmother's. Same prefix, then same digits in a slightly different order. That day, when I rang Alice, or thought I was ringing her, I got this electric voice with an anonymous message followed by a beep. I thought, oh well she can't have sorted the outgoing since moving in, but I'll leave her a message anyway. So I said "Hi, it's me, Nicky. Just to say you're going to be seriously fucked tonight."

You know what's coming next, don't you. You're already there. When I went round in the evening to help her with the unpacking, she said she'd never got any message from me that day and that it couldn't be the machine on the blink as there'd been others left for her. Plus she'd recorded her own outgoing the previous day and it was working fine. I thought back through the digits and it started to dawn on me what I'd done. There was no conclusion possible except I'd left the message on my grandmother's phone.

Then Alice asked me why I was looking so odd, and obviously thought I was on something. She came right up to my eyes and stared into them, like she often does when she thinks I might be pinned. Which I wasn't, and hadn't been for weeks. Although I wouldn't have minded something, I can tell you.

My grandmother wouldn't use her own voice on the outgoing for some weird reason about not wanting to be recognised by people who might not know her. I've never understood all that bollocks, and I stopped trying a long time ago. Anyway, what you got if you called her was one of those standard voices that come with the machine. I knew this because I'd heard Mum mentioning it to her, trying to make a joke of it, poor Mum, and saying "It doesn't sound like you at all, Grandmother Beavis." And then my grandmother, who wouldn't know irony if it bit her up the bum, saying "Well of course it doesn't sound like me, Sheila. It's an automatic voice, it's American and it's male." She said it like it was a complaint at Mum for having given her the machine as a present. You couldn't please her. That was known, like a rule. No pleasing Grandmother Beavis. She was greedy for more and more years, well over her allocation, but wanted to make it clear that she was not enjoying her life and that it was everyone else's fault. Wanting it both ways.

I'm digressing. I could feel the old chaos coming back, a bit like I can now. It seemed unfair, and it still does, seeing as how I hadn't used for all that time and was heading nicely into a long clean period. I tried to slow everything down and get calm, get rational, take it all step by step. It was now about 8.30 on the Saturday night. I suppose it was only a few minutes later that I knew at some level I was going to do the burglary. It all travelled through me in a rush, totally mad, yes, but also totally rational in that madness; it's the way your mind works when you're good and clean, but not for all that long. You've got the brain back, but not the sanity. If you ever had that. So you're wanting to use the brain, drive it about like a car you can be proud of, but the streets aren't behaving. I reckoned I could see the whole likely sequence of the next few hours: getting the spare key to the mansion block - spare keys plural, the front door and the inside; just getting in there and wiping the message from the machine. Removing the whole thing if necessary. I replayed it in my mind. "Hi, it's me, Nicky. Just to say you're going to be seriously fucked tonight." I ran it through my head again and again. In the end it was like talking to myself. It was not as bad as it could have been. Not yet anyway. My grandmother was away in Devon, convalescing. As far as I could remember, she was not due back until the following afternoon, the Sunday. I would have to check that with Mum. I would have to go back round to our house at some stage in the evening. I would need a pretext, like picking up a paintbrush or something. I couldn't just phone from Alice's and ask when my grandmother was due back in London. That would look very suspicious as I never inquired about her movements from one year to the next.

No one ever really knew what she was convalescing from, and everyone was too frightened to ask her directly. I did once raise it with Mum but she became very snappy and told me it was none of my business. So I assumed she was as puzzled as me. Actually I think she was more irritated than puzzled, but was always so worried about "rocking the boat." The phrase came up without fail whenever anyone mentioned my grandmother, or her flat, or her situation, or anything to do with her. If you ask me, convalescence was another word for holiday, but we were all meant to assume she was in a brave and more or less permanent struggle against an unmentionable condition.

It was an anxious time, even more than usual. My grandmother had just made one of her periodic reviews of all her stocks and shares and policies and God knows what. She had brought them up in conversation ever since I was a small boy, and I must have grown up with the idea that these great dark pieces of wealth would one day be mine just as long as I didn't do anything wrong. I was never told what form this wealth would come in, or how much it would add up to, just as I never knew what kind of wrong-doing would put me out of the running for it. The stocks etc. were a powerful implement, because whenever she mentioned them she would glance over at Mum to see what effect it was having, and Mum's face would always turn down like a playing card in a losing hand. If it was just my grandmother and me, she would take me down to the far end of the flat, into the room that had been her husband's study. There she would unlock a drawer in his desk and take out the heavy wads of documents, all faded and folded and tied up with ribbons. A couple of times I remember getting ready to thank her as she seemed on the point of handing them to me. But then they went back in the desk and the drawer was locked. I must have been eight or nine at the time.

My grandfather died when I was two, and all I remember of him is that room with the bare desk and the large model aeroplanes still hanging overhead like giant insects in the fusty air. There was a Sopwith Camel, and a really old one with multiplane wings, and an eight-engine Brabazon as big as an albatross. He had been something important in Hawker-Siddeley, but not as important as she would have liked us all to believe.

The flat was tall and depressing and gave my sister nightmares about animals trapped in falling cages. Even then it was obvious that the animals came from the insect-like planes in the unused room and the cages came from the trellised lift that went slowly up and down in the mansion block.

It was about three weeks ago, just before Alice moved in round the corner, that the business of the inheritance came up again. My grandmother let it be known that I now stood to collect quite a large amount in due course, thanks to the astuteness of the people she had engaged to advise her. Naturally she let this be known through Mum, her daughter-in-law. Grandmother Beavis, said Mum, wished it to be known that her Will was being - what was it? - redrafted in my favour. No, provisionally altered. That was it. I remember the "provisionally," one of those words that kicks in after the first show of generosity, just to let you know it's not all done and dusted quite yet.

When I asked why it was being done this way, Mum just said not to rock the boat. The trouble is - and I'm as embarrassed as I should be about this - the trouble is I could really use the money. I'm twenty three. I'll be twenty four in November. I've hung around too long since I left uni and not really done anything except get wasted and go to interviews where everyone present - me, the main bloke asking questions, everyone else - knows I needn't have bothered to turn up. I suppose I am the embodiment of that joke about what do you say to a philosophy graduate; I don't know, what do you say to a philosophy graduate? Big Mac and fries to go. Har har.

By that night, the night everything happened, I was definitely depressed. Even those weeks away from using didn't make me feel any better. It was actually worse. I was refusing myself permission to have anything that might take the edge off the gloom. It was time to move out of home and think about the future. Mum wasn't exerting any pressure at all. Without having a go at her, I think that was part of the problem. I suppose she didn't want to lose me, having already lost Dad. That was different, of course. He was killed in Recife, in northern Brazil, when I was thirteen. My grandmother maintains he went to the help of some young boys who were being attacked by a street gang. The truth is he was knifed by a pimp after there was a mix-up over currency for a hooker.

I got drunk in Brighton years later with the guy who had been his cameraman. He was down at the uni doing a talk on war photography and I recognised his name from the poster. I went up to him afterwards and said who I was, and late on in the pub I asked him for the truth about what happened. He said my father had never tried to cheat anybody; the light was poor in the hall they were in and he was having trouble with the notes. But he is a hero, my Dad, and that is official. Many times I've wanted to blurt out the real story at table. But it would have hurt Mum badly, which I didn't want to do. Nor for that matter did I want to hurt my grandmother. She was past hurting. As I say, I simply wanted her to shove over and be dead, which is a completely different thing.

I didn't particularly want to hurt myself either. I'm sure it would have been better to have a father who dies as a hero rather than as a philanderer, but I could never really get worked up about it. I'm just pissed off that he died, because he was a good man. It would also have made things a lot easier financially if he'd stayed around, and we wouldn't have to be pieces in my grandmother's power game.

It must have been half past nine when I left Alice's to go back round to our house. I said I would get another paintbrush as her big one was moulting and ruining the fresh walls with stray hairs. She was rather impressed by my commitment to the job. I passed the Leinster and could see all the usual lot in there through the window. I went by like a shutter across a lens and committed the image to my retina for examination as I carried on walking. If they'd seen me they'd have had me in there and it would have been disastrous. Well, I say that. There was Kevin from Cairns, who never had less than ten pints in a night; and old Woody, who was the only regular still allowed a slate; Louise the former model with a name that was something else on other nights; the rock singer from Ipswich; the blind publisher who'd known Joe Orton; and quite a few more of them. They all had that inane, jaws-down and eyes-up look that you get when the TV's come on but it's not yet Match of the Day.

When I got round to our house, there were quite a few people there at the back of the big room. The last daylight had just about gone and I could only see them in silhouette against the French windows. I didn't recognise any of them. There was a powerful smell of spliff and a lot of smoke, and some music which was definitely not my sister's. There was another smell through all this, which was her new going-out perfume. It was hanging on the stairs by the front door, and I thought she must have left. But then there was the pounding which comes from the top of the house when she is running late - fast heavy marching between the bathroom and the bedroom. Then she tips herself at a clatter down the top flight, and by the time she appears she is leaning forward like a ski-jumper with her feet whirring behind her in their big new shoes.

She braked in the hallway, with her face just a few inches from mine. I could see at once that she was suspecting me of something. And I could feel myself looking back at her with what was meant to be a direct look but turned out to be a shifty one. That has always happened between us. She susses me for stuff that has yet to take place, usually to do with drugs or girls. Her expression is meant to make me think she could recite the whole inventory of misdemeanours that I am about to commit. There is a strong back-up look in her eyes, just daring me to call her bluff and go "What then?" which I never do.

That night she was looking specially angry. Obviously Mum wasn't about, hence all the students and their mates doing grass, and so the grief which would have gone her way came mine instead. There's never any words when this happens. There don't have to be. The eyes, the angles, the little movements, they're all going much too quick for language. Words would never keep up here. This is the shorthand of twenty years. I could tell you exactly what she was saying that night in the instant she looked at me before brushing past my shoulder and then off out. She was saying she knew I was getting to something because I had that look, even though I was flaunting the innocence of five or six weeks clean. She was saying why did I have to give her the problem of knowing how Daddy really died? Why did I have to get stoned and give her something so plausible and cross-referenced but which could still have been the product of my sick imagination? She was saying why couldn't I have let it be, instead of setting up this wall of knowledge between us and Mum? She was saying why don't you get a job now you've finished in Brighton? Why aren't there printed envelopes with application forms landing on the mat, same as in other graduates' houses? Why should ours be full of foreign students from loony countries because Mum really had nothing left? She was saying why is it me not her in line for the lion's share of whatever was coming down from our grandmother's dusty old wads of paper? She was saying you've let that woman divide us with the power of an unconfirmed promise. She was saying this is like blackmail in advance.

She was saying the nightmares still come, with the cages and the flying animals, and that she troubles boys with her rages and her silences. She was saying why did you have to be a fucking bloke anyway, and why did your cold tall girlfriend have to come and live so near? All this and more she was saying as she clomped by with her perfume on.

I looked up at the key-hook above the coat rack and there was nothing hanging from it. It was just coming up to 10 o' clock, I could feel the strange advance of panic and futility in me, the one sharp and quite exciting, the other dull and awful. I was tamping them down like tobacco in a pipe. I was making them orderly. I surprised myself with my reason and control.

"Mum's not here," said my sister, gauging my curiosity as accurately as ever. I was meant to say "Oh, where's she gone?" so that she could come back with one of her arch little shrugs. So I just said "right" and tried not to let her see that I could have done with some more information, what with there being nothing on the key-hook. But she wasn't scoring all the points. She lingered in the doorway just long enough for me to sense she didn't quite know what I was about. It was only the fraction of a second, but as I say, that's enough for us.

I know I take the piss, but I can't stand this coldness between us. It's like all the strength in our old closeness is now being used to push us apart; like that force has defected, changed sides. And now that it's against me, against us, I see how strong it is. It's been like this since Alice came along, which is six months now. Alice is long and silky and expensive-looking, which my sister isn't. Just to rub it in, Alice got left a load of money from some old trust and has bought her first house before she's been three months at the agency. It means that all the crap of deposits and flat-sharing and bill-splitting which everyone has to endure has passed her by. Home-wise she's as well in as a professional woman with ten years working life behind her. And all through family money from people she never had to live with. Alice also gets on with Mum, which makes her an arse-crawler in my sister's book.

But worst of all, Alice is called Alice, which happens to be my sister's name as well. It's no-one's fault of course, although my sister would say she got there first (even though she's younger.) If it's logic you want, you don't go looking for it in this area. I did try to make it work between them, between all of us, but it was never a runner. It was hate at first sight, an interplanetary clash of ball-gowns. I tried calling Alice Al, or Ali, and my sister Sis, both as natural as I could make it. When neither of them took, I reverted to calling one of them Alice and the other my sister. Then each of them tried to get me to join them in bad-mouthing the other, which did shock me. Like they were testing me out. Alice was bound to win. Girlfriend versus family is a foregone conclusion. It has to be. Now my sister makes a point of disagreeing with me about everything as a matter of principle. The policy has even made her start declaring her approval for our grandmother. I say, as she used to, that I really don't like the woman, and so she decides that there are real qualities in her "if only you had the courage and perception to get past your own largely generational prejudices."

After my sister had left the house I went through the drawing room towards the kitchen, where the brushes are kept. As I say, I think I had already decided on the burglary, the break-in, call it what you want. I was half way through the drawing room when I realised I didn't know a soul there. And even though they were in silhouette against the French windows, I could tell that not one of them knew who I was either. What with spending so much time away at Alice's, then helping her move in, I didn't even know our own lodgers. My sister had warned me they were dickheads, but she says that about all the students because she had to move into the little back bedroom when Mum started taking them in.

I must have walked between them rather purposefully because I could see them sit up and their shoulders stiffen. It's funny how sensitive you can be to body language when everyone is off their face except you. Behind them the garden was waving and imploring for a small show of affection before summer really was finished. I tried a general "Hi" and got various sounds in return. I heard Japanese, Portuguese, German and something eastern European. Too far east for me to identify. I followed up with "Don't mind me, I only live here," and the Japanese boy took the cue.

"You live in England. Beautiful country."

"Ja, is good," said the German voice, which belonged to a blonde girl with perfect breasts beneath her tee-shirt. The puff, the smell of strange young people among the furniture, their clean limbs in the half-light - it all took me by surprise in the groin and started to make me heavy with blood. I almost made a crack about droit de seigneur, but pulled back just in time. My mother always made a point of taking in Germans and Japanese whenever possible. It was her contribution to burying the great enmities of the century. But it had the added attraction of getting back at her mother-in-law, who still routinely called these nationalities the Ruddy Hun and the Nasty Nip. She never left out the adjectives.

As my eyes accustomed to the gloom, I could see the Japanese boy was translucently beautiful, with serene almond eyes, flawless skin and long shining hair. He smiled at me, and so too did the German girl, with mouths like rare and newly ripened fruits. I guessed they were all first-years and I felt distressingly old. All knackered and crumbling, like our house, like our country. Just about getting by on fresh bullshit and old credit. The Japanese boy wanted to make conversation about the "excellent way" of the British system and went into an unsolicited tract of praise about our facilities for overseas students. At least that's what I think it was, although the conversation then moved without a join into a very positive assessment of our royal family. So much so that I thought it might be a piss-take. We had Mother of the Nation, we had Most Beautiful Woman in the World. These titles went to the Queen Mother and Princess Diana, but there seemed to be some dissent about who got which. We had Wisest of all Men, which I think was the Duke of Edinburgh. Then one of them, a Portuguese girl, started saying "the mother, the mother."

I said "Yes?" and she continued: "She telephone to here."

"The Queen Mother?" I said. "She phoned here?"

The girl saw nothing funny in this and said "No. A sua mao."

"Aha," I said. "Her mother."

"She come back."

"Mother. Old woman."

"Si. Yes."

All of which I took to mean that my grandmother had phoned to remind Mum that her driver would be bringing her back from Devon the next day. This is the kind of thing she would do. There was no particular need for it. She relayed the fact as if it was an important detail in a Court Circular, and also presumably in the hope that Mum would put fresh milk in her fridge or get some flowers in. Mum is a pushover like that.

"She comes home," the Portuguese girl repeated.

"Out on date," said one of the others, who had not yet spoken. He was sitting cross-legged on the floor and was very obviously stoned.

"Jiggy-jiggy" he said, making a thrusting gesture with his pelvis and drawing himself forward several inches like a yogic leaper. There was a silence and then everyone started giggling. To begin with they made a token effort to suppress the laughter, but it was no use. It never is when you are in that state. I tried to smile as well, to show them it was OK, but they were looking at each other in the way that excludes everyone else. The laughter died down a little, then the German girl said "Jiggy-jiggy" and wiggled on her chair, and it started up again.

I got it, of course I got it. The thought of an old woman out on a shagging mission. Always a good one that, when you're out of it. Except it was, after all, my grandmother they were using for their ridicule. Maybe they didn't know where I fitted in. Maybe they just didn't care. And I thought, wait a minute, she's my sodding relative, I'll do the jokes thank you very much. The red mist was falling on me. I suppose I could have lost it badly if I'd been using. Or maybe not. Maybe I'd have laughed along with them. Maybe I'm only losing it now because I'm not using. God knows. I've lost it for less than that in the past.

Instead I went into a strange kind of focus: get the paintbrush from the kitchen, and out. No point in asking them if they knew where the keys from the hook had gone. No point at all. I got the brush from the cupboard, and some white spirit for when Alice got round to the gloss. When I passed back through between them they were laughing uncontrollably. Anything was setting them off. This time one of them was pointing to a CD cover on the floor, and finding something hysterically funny. It was an old Stranglers album. There were others in a scatter next to it: Madness, Talking Heads, Police, all mine from when I was a kid. It was like these people were laughing at my taste or, worse still, laughing at the taste of the kid I used to be.

I left feeling weird and raging, and took a sweet, plain lungful of the August night. It tasted very English in that way the air can. From an open window across the road there was the sound of a football crowd going Ooooo!! at a near miss.

Then I was thinking about the family, about the way I could almost close ranks with this dreadful relative of mine when someone from outside is having a go. I was thinking how my sister and I have always spared Mum the details of why we dislike the old woman so much; and how strange that is, seeing as she's not even her mother but her mother-in-law, which could not be more different. It's all to do with not dirtying anything connected with Dad.

It would be easier if she weren't such a professional in the business of being unspeakable. I agree that when people are up in their eighties and still very much batting, it can be a source of inspiration to other people. I've no problem with that. But this isn't batting. This is hogging the crease and not letting anyone else in; not allowing the existence of any other opinion, and therefore not of any other generation. So it's always been: "Well, Nicholas, I expect it will be engineering for you." Or else: "Have you been in touch with Stewart's old college? I'm sure they'd be delighted to have you." And asking me questions about school as if I was at Harrow. Asking me about Latin masters for heaven's sake, and me having to make one up. Her just not understanding the notion of philosophy as a course; hearing the word and then somehow dismissing it as an illusion or error on my part. Even after Sussex she would say: "Will it be the city for you then, Nicholas?" And there's me with a head all fucked over by Wittgenstein, and a job market all fucked over by forces of equal obscurity. Always that disdain of hers, coming down as heavy as the lift. Knocking new things, rejecting them like food done wrong. It's a sending-back mentality. Send back the new people, the new ideas, the new times, they'll never be a patch on what used to be. Always that uncompleted promise of what was hers and will be mine. It's yours, she would say. It's yours but it's not yours. The same as the Royals, isn't it. Being so very for us, but not really when it comes down to it. Subject is such a telling word, meaning thrown underneath. That's why I say shove over.

As I passed the open door of the Leinster, Arsenal were on the wrong end of a decision and everyone was baying "Refereeeee!" at the television. An arm came out of the door and crooked me in. Before I knew it I was in the dark of the bar, with my face looking up at the screen and someone forcing a beer into my hand. It all happened in a single movement, like a fish being whipped in and processed. If an authority on London told you that it was a sequence which had evolved to perfection over millennia, you would have to believe him. The arm belonged to Kevin. It was brown and sinuous and felt stronger than all of me put together. He could shift vast quantities of beer and still look as fit as a surfer. I normally hate people like that. The instant pint came from him as well. It was there on the bar, waiting for his attention in a queue of three.

Before I could remind him, or me, that I was off everything at present, including drink, it had gone down and there was another being inched forward at me towards the edge of the bar. Seaman was under a spot of pressure from the Spurs strikers. Then he outjumped Les Ferdinand to gather a high cross and everyone went "Spunkeee! Spunkeee!" - the home crowd in the North Stand, the boys in the family seats, and people like us in the Leinster. We should have been a Chelsea pub, being in West London, and I think we once were, back in the days of Chopper Harris and Peter Osgood, before it all went precious and imported down at Stamford Bridge. There was only one of us in the Leinster that night who was a Spurs supporter, and that was the blind publisher, Landon. As he couldn't see anything he just went "Football, Spurs, football," no matter what was going on or how loud everyone was shouting.

It was past eleven when the match ended in a goalless draw. The barman was shouting "Your very last orders now please," which was the cue for our bunch to settle in for some After Hours. Woody had a large brandy put on his slate, and without asking him the barman extended the round to take in the rest of us. When you're sober, you do see how the barmen take advantage of the drinkers. Kevin's queue of beers was vanishing with its usual late burst, and the model had moved on to Gin-and-Its. Kevin told me to relax and not look so worried. I went deep into the second pint, still without thinking. Because of being clean all these weeks, and barely even doing cigarettes, I had totally lost my tolerance. It does get a little blank here, but I must have said something about the rude message trapped in my grandmother's flat, and my plan to burgle the mansion block. I'm surprised it made any sense, but Kevin must have got it in one. Before I could say anything else he was steering me over into the darkness at the back of the pub and introducing me to a man who was guaranteed to solve my problem for me. I got the impression Kevin already had some professional association with him because he approached him rather formally and respectfully.

"Manny, I'd like you to meet a friend of mine, Nicky Beavis. Nicky, this is Manny Weinmann."

"Pleased to meet you, Nicky," said Manny.

"Me too."

"Won't you sit down."

"Can't I get you a drink first?"

"In time."

I sat opposite him while the rest of the pub moved towards the bar like a late tide making up the ground. Manny was a slight man in his late thirties or early forties. He was wiry, with the texture of a jockey, and already I imagined him getting through tiny cracks in windows and twisting himself among properties via the waste ducts.

I started explaining the situation to him, all the time apologising for the implausibility of it. I had a spot trouble believing it myself as I was telling him. He waved the apologies away to show he understood perfectly and had heard far stranger things. "Sometimes," he said, "it is a mistake to explain too much." In any other company I might have taken issue with him and said the whole problem with the English was they didn't explain enough but always expected other people to guess.

He asked me some questions about the flat, and I was able to answer most of them. When I told him the name of the block he nodded in recognition. Perhaps he'd done some work there before. He said to come back and meet him here at the Leinster later on. It was now well gone 11.00. Chelsea/Southampton was on, Petrescu had just knocked in the first goal for the Blues, and no-one in the Leinster was particularly happy. Landon was still going "Football, Spurs, football."

"Later on?" I said.

"Yes," said Manny. "Any time. Just come to the front door. We see you through the glass."

I thanked him and hurried off round to Alice's. Instead of giving me a hard time for having taken so long, she was very grateful for the brush, and even more so for the white spirit.

"This is really very clever of you, Nicky."

"It's only white spirit," I said.

"Yes, but you must have read my mind."

I think I might have done, without knowing it. The thing about Alice is that she is totally into whatever it is that she's doing. That's why she's always done so well at anything she chose - exams, swimming, men - and it's why she'll make such a go of her business life. Everyone knows this. It's not a matter of whether she'll make a million, only when. Will it be twenty seven, or will she have to wait until twenty nine?

Just for the moment she was into painting. And because I had thought of something she needed, I was good news. I do sometimes wonder how long I can hang on to her. She doesn't seem to have any great need for me, or anyone else. It does make a change, with my record, and I think it's definitely what keeps me wanting her. Maybe she's just clever. Maybe I'll do till something better comes along.

With the benefit of hindsight, it was a mistake to request a fuck at this point. I don't know what was going on. I think the notion of a mission with Manny was turning me on. The fear and everything. I'd outed myself to him, and now I had to go through with it. The thing had its own dynamic, never mind it was barking. The nerves were making me randy, and the beer was taking the edge off my inhibitions. Plus - and this is important - I was reasoning it was a sound idea to be a bit demonstrative now. It was a good insurance move against anything unpopular that might happen later on. For a start, I hadn't thought through whether I would be straight, and say I was going back round to the pub later, or whether I would say I was off home to keep an eye on things in Mum's absence. The second option was looking favourite.

Anyway, in about two minutes all our clothes were off and we were down on the bed base, with the mattress still leant up out of the way. You sometimes forget how nice it can be to fuck on a firm surface. In no time at all she was shouting and tossing, and I thought this isn't going to be a duty-shag at all. It's funny how it goes. Some of the longest-planned ones, like years, turn out to be the most disappointing. And then one which five minutes before wasn't in your mind at all blows the top of your head off.

I started shouting as well, and rolling off the bed base onto the floor. Both our heads tapped against the skirting board, and I think it was here that it all went pear-shaped. The shouting stopped and she turned all awkward around me, pushing my ribs away with her hands in the Halt! position. As quickly as it had started, it was over. She'd stopped shouting and so I did as well. You can't really carry on at volume when the other person's gone silent. A few more seconds and I'd been disconnected like an appliance. She was on her feet, with the small paintbrush in her hand. Then she was bending down to touch up the skirting board where we had messed the fresh paint with our heads.

She didn't seem angry or anything, she just needed to get on with the job. She was more absorbed by this than men by football. I might not have been there. She didn't even look up until it was all smoothed over, and when she did I could see she had a badger-tuft of white on the front of her hair, and was pointing at mine to make a similar observation. Then she carried on round to the next wall. There was no point my asking her how long she would be at it as the answer was she didn't know. My guess was she was digging in for the night, and that's why she thought it was a diplomatic investment to fuck me first. In addition, I would say she was off her face with paint fumes. My mission, her painting. My booze, her fumes. There was a kind of balance. As I got dressed I found we had landed in a small row. She was accusing me of having a dodgy relationship with my sister, and so I said the same about her and her father. As she wouldn't explain what she meant, I refused to as well, although I did say she knew perfectly well what I was talking about (I certainly didn't have a clue myself), and I could see that rattle her.

Then I walked out and she made one of her jungle noises. The evening was like a compressed cycle of the relationship business: supportive, affectionate, stoned, shagging, not shagging, hungover, resentful, lying, leaving. The short-term gain for me was my right to liberty for the night. I went back round to the Leinster, this time taking a longer route and spending an age going backwards and forwards in front of the mansion block, looking up at the pipes and windows, sizing the place up for distances and drops. My heart worked so hard that it made everything race round and left me dead sober. Manny recognised my silhouette through the glass, as he said he would, and opened the door.

They were all still there: Kevin still drinking pints, and right as ninepence; old Woody, still racking it up on the slate; the rock-singer from Ipswich, worse for wear now and trying not to say anything; Louise, the former model; Landon the blind publisher; and Manny Weinmann himself. There was another table with a similar number, over in the front, directly under the TV. The screen was silent now. There was a film on with famous American actors twenty five years ago, all wearing seventies hair and broad lapels. It was being interrupted by an urgent man in a dark street. Something was happening in the world, but no-one else was interested, and the film came back again. The guy was Donald Sutherland, looking so like Kiefer, and the girl underneath him was Jane Fonda, looking a little like Bridget. It was now well after 1.00 a.m. and we were all heading into the unmapped area of the night.

"Ah Nicky, what's yours," said Woody. "I'm just doing the shopping."

I decided to take it easy and have a Coke. Someone made a joke about whether I wanted it up the nose, and although Woody and Landon laughed along with the others I swear they had no idea what it was about. The men at the other table were playing dominoes, keeping the scores in rows of upright matchsticks. There was a Trinidadian called Granville, who always won.

A smell of cooking came through from the kitchen, and then the sound of fat food spitting. The heavy old Alsatian came out from the bar on a routine inspection. It felt like breakfast, and I wondered if the night had compressed itself, like my dealings with Alice, and passed without me clocking it. I also wondered if Manny had done the mission and now I would have to scroll back through the flown hours if I wanted a recollection of it. But it was somewhere in the twos. I tried to look at other watches, and there was a rough consensus of half past. The urgent man in the street came back onto the screen. Then the whole thing went snowy, like a system crashing in the downtime. Granville stood up and switched it off. There was night jazz coming from a tinny radio in the kitchen, and from time to time a French voice saying English names.

Manny smiled cosily at me. I tried to stifle the anxiety in my face. I had so much to ask. I felt sheltered and conventional. I was an embarrassment. How do we do it? Is it a ladder job? Ropes? Will there be a charge for this, and if so how much?

Old Woody and Blind Landon liked having me in the Leinster. I think they felt it raised the intellectual tone because I could say words like Heidegger, praxis or Schopenhauer without turning a hair. After a few pints I could put words like that together into long sentences and be perfectly confident that they were rubbish from beginning to end. It's not exactly that I was showing off. I wasn't. It's just that they took such pleasure in hearing these things from someone (me) who assumed they understood but who yet made no demands on them- it flattered them and entertained them, and I hated to let them down. I thought of my so-called tutor at Sussex. I hardly ever exchanged a word with him while I was there, mainly because I never understood a word he was saying. I think that was the idea. One day someone in our group asked him if our course had any practical application at all in the world beyond, and he replied that its purpose would make itself known at times and in places we could not predict. There in the Leinster that night, I think I got it.

Landon shuffled his face as he always did when he was about to make important conversation. Eventually, after a lot of painful consideration, he said "Treitschke." I waited for the rest of the statement, but there was nothing more. Having said the word, he fell silent again and took a swig of beer. I think the idea was for me to pick up the proposition and play with it. It was the bone to my dog. Unable to think of anything to contribute, I said "Ah yes," trying to make it sound as though Landon and I had an understanding on the subject. I don't think I'd ever done Treitschke. And if I had I'd forgotten it, just as I'd forgotten most of the Europeans. They'd all fused into a general up-its-arse rant about God being an old fraud. A police car went whooping by in the next street, throwing a quick blue flash onto the ceiling above us, and Manny Weinmann gave me another affectionate smile.

The singer from Ipswich asked if I was into relativity, and started to explain how, if we travelled away from the earth faster than light, we could witness events that had taken place in the past. It meant that somewhere out there tomorrow, radiating away at a colossal rate, there would be a permanent visual record of me breaking into my grandmother's flat tonight. A souvenir video, available from stores not very near you. From the same team that didn't bring you *Alfred Burns the Cakes* and *Drake Sinks the Don*.

He agreed there would be some difficulty accessing the evidence, but didn't see it as a major problem long-term. Once again I began to ponder the closer mystery of how, in a relatively short life, I could already have spent so many light years trading hot air in dark pubs.

Woody did some more shopping and I had another Coke. He referred to it as The Boy's Snort, without knowing how witty this might have been. The beer had worn right off now and the nerves spotted an opening. These nothing-hours took me back eight years to being a graffiti boy along the depots of the Central Line. There were nearly as many of us in our gang then as there were men around this table now. Me, Gavin, Johnny, Kit and Xavier. It was the same tension while you drifted in the time, waiting for it to deepen properly off the mainland shelf of day. The same knot and sickness, and knowing they wouldn't go away until the mission was done. You weren't a real writer till you'd pieced a train. All the rumours about what the guard dogs did in the Transport Police. Talk of kids' heads being found four hundred yards from their bodies. The ridiculous loyalty that would have made you walk through fire before you grassed. The utter solidarity in the face of...of whatever force would try to keep you from the business. The smells of the sleeping trains at White City or out at Ealing. The deafening acrid of the aerosols and the beautiful shapes emerging like butterflies or draped moths. The snatch of the flash-bulb and the big proud Tag printing itself into your blinded eyes. The running off and waiting for the morning. The sighting of your carriage as it went painted on its long way to Epping. Where on earth was Epping? The world stopping when Xavier caught a live rail and kicked himself to death with sparks.

I glanced up at Manny Weinmann. He smiled and nodded, just like he'd been listening to all this babble and understood perfectly. I thought of all the time that had passed since those days, not slowly but like the wind. One minute I was younger than the students back at the house, next minute my youth is history. I thought of the useless stuff tipping like effluent from my head by the week. Half-learnt systems of thought, laid down by madmen and now fading into the faintness of a fourth or fifth carbon. The futility of it, in these of all times. Stuck in the Leinster talking crap. Junior Lecturer in the University of Life. Then I thought of the young pilots in the war films, waiting for the hours to pass. Was this travesty the best I could come up with? What a waste of a generation it was.

The clocks had now dragged themselves past three, the time when the hands feel their weight and get their first inkling of a downhill run. The big dog came round again and startled me more than he meant to. With the exception of Manny and me, everyone at the table was now asleep. The silent singer and the former model were leaning against each other like bookends. Woody had his mouth slightly ajar as if it was just about to alert the barman to a new outbreak of thirst. Blind Landon was bolt upright and motionless. So was Kevin, who was still standing at the bar. I imagined they would all remain like this until the light caught them in the morning and they would carry on where they had left off.

"Very well then, Nicky," said Manny, and got to his feet. We passed between the ash-people-of-Pompeii scene and let ourselves quietly out into the street. It was empty and lifeless, but not entirely so. I don't think the London streets are ever one hundred per cent without people these days. We set off for the mansion blocks, using the route that takes you past the end of Alice's mews. I was half-expecting Manny to have a van parked down there with his gear. He didn't seem to have anything on him at all - no tackle of any description. I imagined Alice coming out of her house, spotting us and then shopping me to the police as a means of emerging victorious from our stand-off.

To my surprise Manny actually swung right at this point and we went straight down into the mews itself. I always forget you can get through to the mansion blocks along the little footpath at the end. There were the usual smattering of lights on in the homes of the night owls and insomniacs. Alice's of course, with its shadeless bulb and uncurtained window, was the brightest. We passed bang underneath and there she was, still in her dungarees, unstoppable and pissed on paint, her arm waltzing to and fro on its roller across the opposite wall. I ducked my head and hurried on. Manny said "no worries Nicky" and we dipped between the house-backs at the end of the news, then funnelled out into my grandmother's street barely two hundred yards from her main entrance.

At some time in the night - it could have been here or it could have been back in the Leinster - I know I started querying the sanity of my plan. (Or Manny's plan as I should now call it.) I was late off the mark here, I know, but I did do some querying. I was asking myself if it might not have been more sensible to try and leave some corrective message on the old woman's machine, explaining that the previous one had been a poor joke by an unwell friend of mine; or else I could have just filled the whole tape with a blank message and hoped she wouldn't wind back to the beginning. But it was half-hearted querying. I was with Manny now and that was that. The world has no shortage of top pros who'll do the whackiest things for you and make it seem quite normal.

There was a young couple snogging in one of the broad doorways. It was probably her parents' place. When they broke off she looked at him pleasantly but discouragingly, like she had come to the end of what was on offer for the moment. Poor bloke, I thought. It's yours, but it's not yours.

There was still the sound of traffic coming from the big roads away to the left. Not isolated cars, but traffic. Somewhere nearer there was a car alarm whinging elaborately and no-one taking any notice. They're a disgusting trend, those drama queen Euroboxes. There was no second-guessing Manny. I think that for him that's where the kicks came in. For all I knew, he was about to go up, vertical as a Harrier, and then just step across the air onto the fourth floor balcony. I also had no idea what was being expected of me. It was a bit like being led up to the top of a very high diving tower, with the real possibility of having to go off.

"This one?" he said when we came level with the entrance.

I nodded. It was a great bulbous block of red brick, built at the turn of the century to accommodate the aspirations of the merchant class. I remember my grandmother saying that it had been built when the Queen Mother was a baby and before Victoria had died. I don't know if she thought this lifted it even further from the commonplace, but for me it meant that the whole fussy bulk of it was forever linked with indomitable old women. It was as forbidding as any castle, but without the compensation of irregularities. It just marched down the length of the street being important.

Among its mass, outside and in, there was not a chink of legitimacy for animals, or children, or any other agent of noise. No gardens, just a dull belt of tiles and square-potted shrubs patrolling the front. No wonder my sister and I had felt such fear at the prospect of it, such wrongness in the body of it. Accommodation was only half the story. The real game was exclusion.

So it was really very surprising when Manny simply opened the great fuck-off front door and there we were standing in the hall under the high ceiling. By the light in here I could see a bunch of keys beneath his jacket. It was the size of a substantial growth, or small beehive, yet when he walked it hung from the inside of his clothes without any protrusion. He was ready for my obvious question. So ready that I didn't have to ask it.

"How I knew which key for this lock, eh Nicky?"

I nodded.

"Because," he said, "I know." He realised it was an answer that called for a little after-sales service, and so he provided it. "You know your Mr. Hegel and your Mr. Humple, OK? and I know my business too."

There were at least two errors, one of them potentially grave. First, if his knowledge of his business was on a par with my knowledge of what he took to be my business, then we were already looking at twelve months minimum without nicking so much as an ashtray. Secondly, there was no such philosopher as Humple, unless Manny actually knew more about it than I did. Quite possible.

"Touch nothing and don't act guilty," he instructed. "So we're in your grandmother's block of flats. So big deal." The lift was absent up the shaft, and I found myself looking at that terrible black hole behind the trellis of the outer door. My imagination began to regress, just as I had feared it would. Any moment now I would hear the heavy clunk of the motor starting up in the heart of the masonry and the lift would bring its prey down in its mouth.

To mount the stairs here was always to feel you had committed some offence and were going up for penance. So nothing new. The stairs were broad and shallow, with the same thick maroon carpet that had always been there. It was virtually unworn, having only had to bear the tread of slow and elderly people who decided against the lift. It was not a great traffic.

"Do you mean to say," I whispered, "that you can get in anywhere you want?"

Manny put his hand out flat and half-rotated it on his wrist to denote "more or less." But his choice of key for the block had been so instant that it was making me wonder whether he was already on familiar terms with the premises. A couple of years ago there had been some burglaries which were so smooth and clever that no-one was ever caught. This was not a good moment to raise the subject. It could easily be taken for ingratitude. Instead I tried to enjoy the power of Manny's professionalism and to imagine myself in possession of his passe-partout skills, gliding into private or public interiors as and when I chose. Here was a man to know.

I also tried to persuade myself that I was not engaged in anything wrong, only trying to head off the damage that would be caused by an innocent error. But the self-advocacy was not working. The place was not congenial to mercy and light judgements.

On the last few steps up to my grandmother's door I had a truly dreadful foreboding. It wrapped me up like all the worst dreams I have ever had about the mansions, all rolled into one. As with those dreams, my voice was nowhere to be found. So before I could put any kind of utterance together, we were in. Two Ingersolls, a Chubb and something else. My grandmother was as greedy for security as she was for years. It used to take her half a morning to undo all that hardware, leaning down over it like a swotty girl covering up her sums.

The moment we were in I could tell that something was wrong, that things had happened which I was totally unprepared for. The entrance gives into the flat's own high hallway, with doors going off it to either side. If you carry on down the hall it does a sharp right angle and then goes down towards the fusty study with the hanging aircraft and the wads of legacy paper. Our objective, the drawing room with the telephone, was two-thirds of the way along that cul-de-sac.

The first room, the one immediately to our right, has rarely been used. You automatically went past its closed door after entering the flat. It was one of the areas that was kept away from general access. Usage, or the lack of it, had placed it out of bounds. I reckoned that nearly half the rooms of the flat were in that same shadowy status - never dirty, never rumpled, never heated, but just remaining as they had been for so long, full of blame, empty of men, too stiff to mourn openly. It's no wonder my voice stayed unavailable when I saw that the door of this first room was slightly open, that the light was on inside and that there were voices coming from it. One of the voices sounded just like Mum's. The other was a light male voice, surely the same one that had been calling our house and asking whether she was in. But they sounded a little muted and artificial. Maybe that was the acoustic of the horrible flat again. Maybe it had the power to make honest sounds turn false.

Then they stopped. All this was happening in a very few seconds, just like when

I see my sister. The picture might seem to be hanging there for ever, but really it's over just like that. I guessed the voices had stopped because they had heard the click of the door, in just the same way me and Manny froze in the hall when we heard the voices in the room. This was just like the graffiti days, just like going rigid in the depot when you see a light flashing close to you. It has to be the Transport Filth with a torch, when more likely it's just some geezer on a bike way over beyond the railings. But while it is the Filth and everything has to work itself out, you're stuck like a stiff and you're living in eternity.

So there we were, Manny and me, rooted to the hall carpet, and this time him looking to me for a lead. Well, his part of the work was technically over. He'd got us in, and what a breeze it had been. A total clear round, Murray Walker lost for superlatives. Now it was me in the frame. No more Mr. Passenger. I was David Niven in *Guns of Navarone*. We'd all got up to the emplacement but I'd yet to justify my ticket and stiff the gun. I did what I've always done; tried to slow it right down and take it step by step. So Mum had got a boyfriend. This was good. And he sounded very nice on the phone. And like bold girls throughout history she was using her mother-in-law's place for a shag. "A sua mao." Sua. The Portuguese student back at the house had emphasised that word. Possessive pronoun or whatever it was. It could mean yours as well as hers. "Your mother rang." So Mum had rung to say she would be back. Meaning she would be out before that. Hence no keys on the hook. Good for Mum. I hope I get on with him. She deserves it. But will he take my room?

Gradually everything did start to settle down, and a solution came marching out of the murk like a man in white. The truth. There was nothing wrong with the truth. I find this can be a startling discovery, but it's beautiful when it happens. After we'd all got through the shock of finding each other there, I would explain to Mum exactly what I'd done and the steps I'd taken to put it right and spare Grandmother Beavis's feelings. I would introduce her to Manny, she would introduce me to whatever her boyfriend was called, and it would all be fine. After the initial shock, which would admittedly be great.

When I looked again at the door, it seemed to open into a room much larger than was possible. Appreciating the thickness of the carpet for the first time, I edged my way a little nearer and realised that the impression was caused by a large mirror on the wall at right angles to the door. I now had a significantly broader view of the room sent back to me in reflection. The voices remained silent. In their place came a third one, which was not familiar. There was a television on. I went still closer to the door to broaden the view further. One thing I could not do was alarm them with their clothes off. I really didn't fancy that.

There was someone on the screen against an obscure background of night streets. I recognised him. It was the urgent man who had come on while we were still round at the Leinster. There were now more lights behind him than before, and some people had gathered in the corners of the picture. He looked as if he was struggling against his own words, and not really trusting them as he sent them out through the microphone. "And so, if these first reports are accurate, we must prepare ourselves for the tragic news that Diana, Princess of Wales, is dead. This is Somebody Somebody, Somewhere Somewhere, in Paris."

Then there was a sequence of shots of Diana - toddler on a swing, gangling girl at Althorp, ultimate bride, doe-eyed charity megastar, Dodi's girlfriend, defiant now rather than bashful. Brassy almost. Self-reclaiming Nineties woman. Not much talking now, but something a bit clipped about how she'd been planning to emigrate. That's it, I thought. She's off to live in one of those fairy tale palaces of Fayed's. They've bought her up and exported her. Fine by me. And when they say dead, of course they don't mean it literally. That's the story: Di Quits Brits for Dodi. It had been such a silly season after all. Nothing in the papers all summer except for Spice Girls garbage and duff alien sightings. No wonder they're going big with this one. And it's a good excuse to roll the old footage.

But then the man came on the screen again, looking grimmer than ever. He said it again: "Princess Diana is believed to have died at the Saint Pitière Hospital this morning." So I thought, it's a drugs death. She's topped herself. Maybe not on purpose, but it's a cry for help that's gone all the way. Then the man began referring to a piece of paper which he'd just been handed, and reading the names of Alain Paul, who was driving the car she was in, and Trevor Rhys-Jones, who was her bodyguard. Both these men were at least critically ill and may be dead, he said, as was Dodi Al Fayed.

While all this was going on, I forgot about where I was standing, or why, or with whom. The broadcast cut back to a studio in London, where a man and a woman were talking in low voices. It was the two who from the other side of the door I had taken to be Mum and her companion. So who...

The thought that Princess Di was probably dead filled me with a terrible thrill. Terrible because it was so big and so devilishly strong. It's not that I was glad, because I wasn't. In fact I knew I was going to be badly saddened in my own small way. It's just that it was so very, very, the only word is thrilling. There's no point in denying it, and I know I'm not the only one who felt that way. I'm certainly not going to pretend that I went all brave and dewy and thought about the greatness of our nation or the Spencer family's tragic heritage or the splendour of our National Parks. Some people do.

Manny, standing half in and half out of the room, said: "Well, that was always in the script," and left it at that. This was early days, early seconds. It would need some absorbing. I remembered that from my father's death. Such bald words, such a long tunnel of consequences stretching off into the distance like a wrong-ended telescope. Where were you when Diana died? I was burgling my grandmother's flat with a strange man.

It was a couple more seconds before I remembered there was someone else in the room. I glanced over my shoulder to the settee, where someone watching the TV would sit, but it was empty. Or very nearly empty. What I did see failed to register properly first go. I think anything would have failed to make its presence felt, given the competition it was up against. That was always Diana's knack while she was alive, and she wasn't abandoning it now. It could have been the Queen Mother sitting there with a G and T in her hand and I would still have missed it.

There was now some lady biographer on the line from Chicago. She was talking about how Diana had taken the city by storm. She was managing to speak clearly and cry all at the same time in a way the English still can't match. Oh, it was going to be such a monster story. We hadn't seen anything yet. Everyone would be blaming everyone else for having killed her.

It wasn't the Queen Mother in the room with me, but it was the closest thing we could manage in our little set-up. Her chin was resting on the arm of the sofa, and the remainder of her was slumped on the floor next to it. She was sort of crumpled down onto herself, with only the face visible. She was very relaxed, and did not look as if she had fallen into that position, although clearly she had done. Not dead though, surely. I know she was a great royalist, but this was overdoing the idea of coming out in sympathy.

It gets very difficult here, because ever since then I've got two versions of what happened next. I wish it weren't confused in this way, but it is. If someone assured me it is possible to see double in a temporal sense - that is, to be presented with alternative images of the same moment - I would be tempted to believe them. It is rich, considering that at this point I was not by any definition stoned.

These were the two things I saw or didn't see. First, her catching me full in the eyes with hers, looking at me with the pitch of reproach you keep for people who've wrecked your life: and then moving a little. I would describe it as a nestling motion in her features, and a taking in of breath ready to say something. Then giving up on the effort, letting the air go and leaving all the communicating work to the eyes. That was one version.

The other was her doing nothing at all. Essence of zero, even with the open eyes. Just flatlining her way through the encounter. But I could tell she was looking at me, even if she didn't think she was. At the end of both these versions, on the resumption of normal time, someone on the telly said, "It's the photographers that have killed her," and I was thinking, that's funny, why would the photographers have wanted to bump off my grandmother? Me I can understand. But photographers?

I heard myself say, "But Grandmother Beavis you're still in Devon." I've always used her full-out title for the first address, because she goes sour if you don't, and then I'd drop it down to plain Grandmother.

There was a noise of something in the street. Not the street on the telly this time, but the street below us. It might have been an urban fox in pain, but it sounded too human. A very late drunk perhaps, all stale and rejected, and dragging himself home like a piece of shit.

By this time Manny was fully in the room. He'd lost whatever small interest he'd had in the T.V. It might as well have been showing Open University calculus. He glanced down at my grandmother with his head to one side in an assessing manner. He looked very game, but then very daunted, as if he knew this was a job he didn't have the key for.

Next he looked up at me. I was aware of my face asking an unreasonable number of questions. He went right up close to her, jutting out his ear like a very attentive listener. Then he felt down for her right wrist on the other side of the settee arm, and looked thoughtfully ahead of him. I noticed the remote control unit was in her hand. He took it from her and handed it to me. My hand recoiled at the last minute and it fell to the floor. I thought how unimpressed she was by his attentions. Surly and graceless. Without a doubt she would think him common and want a minimum to do with him. That was always her phrase. "A minimum to do with him." Or her, or it. I was going to be embarrassed by my family again. And here was Manny, selfless, courteous, professional, and, as far as I could tell, not wanting a penny from me for his services. Or not yet.

Eventually he said, "Hmmm" and stood up. I felt I should be offering a bit more in the way of support, but all I could manage was "What d'you think then?" I don't know why I expected him to know about any of these things. I suppose I started from the certainty that I knew nothing and then I reckoned, very wishfully, that his line of work might have taken him into these situations. It's how I used to feel at Brighton when I was in someone's car and it broke down on the Downs - useless, a luxury, full of dud thoughts on dialectical materialism and logical positivism. I could see from Manny's face that he was not going to get my grandmother started again.

"What I think," he said, answering my question slowly and with due weight, "what I think is, bottom line, Nicky, more Heaven than Devon."

By now some big names were being alerted to the events in Paris. There were a couple of old politicians who had been acting dead themselves for years and who now came alive to express their grief. They were loving it. All those double-breasted suits and tastefully venal faces, technically handsome forty years ago, doing the churchy voice and the compassionate eyes. Classy mourning on the nation's behalf. One of them I could have sworn was a republican firebrand not long ago, an essential weapon in all assaults on the Civil List.

As the reactions to Diana were arriving in the television, so the questions about my grandmother were assembling themselves in my head. How? When? How long?

Why? Not very original questions, I admit, but the relevant ones all the same. I knew I ought to do as Manny had one - touch her to see how cold she was. That's what people did in films, even quite reputable ones. As I had never been able to touch her in her lifetime, and made sure my kisses went off a long way from her face, it was still unthinkable now. I could put a spoon against her, hold it there and then see if it was warm.

Of course I was trying to slow it down, but it wasn't helping. It just meant that each hideous second was lasting longer than it would otherwise have done. Besides, there was a nightmare conclusion presenting itself to me at its own pace. Manny must have read my thoughts because he went off to look for the answerphone and carry out the original purpose of our mission. He must have had some trouble with the drawing room door, as I heard the clanking of his great bunch of keys again, and eventually the sound of a cylinder lock opening. I had forgotten about my grandmother's habit of locking internal doors.

It was while he was in the drawing room that the others arrived. This happened more than quickly. One minute there was no-one here except for Manny and me, and of course my grandmother; the next there was Mum, plus the man with the familiar voice, plus two Filth, a PC with a face like an actor and a stocky young WPC who I would not have liked to tangle with. They must have come straight up the stairs and in through the still-open door of the flat. Mum looked down at Grandmother Beavis, then back up at me. In fact they all did. Mum's face was a give-away. She was shocked. Naturally she was. It is always shocking to come into a room and find a dead person. But there was the other side of the story in her eyes as well. The side of the unexpressable thrill. Softly and matter-of-factly she said "Grandmother Beavis," like she was identifying the body for the PC. She wasn't letting the shock show. She was absorbing it for later. For her, same as for me, there was something plain unbelievable about seeing the old woman in that position, so totally abased, so empty of judgement and complaint. She still managed to look disapproving, that goes without saying; still liable to observe that the waitress's skirt was far too short, or that there were many more black people in Bayswater than was necessary.

I looked at Mum's face again. It was full of sadness and gladness, both of them going deep back into her expression in alternating layers. It made her look soft and very beautiful. I could see what this boyfriend of hers saw in her. It had to be a boyfriend, although I hadn't had time to clock him properly. I wondered if she was savouring, as I was, the posture in which her crippling mother-in-law had passed from the estate of breath and movement. It was a position of prayer, atonement, and ultimate defeat.

Sensing some action elsewhere in the flat, the PC went off down the hall. When he returned he had Manny with him and was holding the little cassette from the answering machine. Manny was looking at me as if to apologise, and I tried to dismiss it with my face. It was me who should be feeling the guilt, and I was, I was.

"Look who we've got here," said the P.C. to his colleague. He sounded more sociable than clever-copper.

"Oh hello, Manny," she said, also rather friendly.

I reckoned I could tell what had happened, and I turned out to be pretty close to the truth. My grandmother had been ringing and ringing the house the previous day. She had fallen out with someone in Devon (she never restricted this activity to family) and managed to get the chauffeured car to drive her all the way back to London on Saturday. She had not been able to communicate this change of plan as Mum had been out with her bloke and the phone kept being answered by stoned students from abroad.

A sua mao. The possessive pronoun. Sua could be second person singular as well as third. A sua mao. Your mother. The Portuguese student was telling me Mum had rung to say she'd be home later. And then when she'd got home in the evening, presumably with the bloke, she must have got her own message back from one of the other students, as well as a garbled version of Grandmother Beavis's intentions. It was not until the small hours, when Mum went on one of her night walks downstairs and saw the keys missing from the hook that she suddenly had a panic. She's always managed to conjure up dire emergencies in her imagination, as anxious parents do with their young children. Always fearing her mother-in-law has fallen prey to a mugger (possible), a rapist (impossible) or a burglar (no comment). What with the combination of confused messages, no word from Grandmother Beavis and the spare key gone awol, Mum started drowning in the panic and phoned the Filth. And now here they all were, with the boyfriend still in tow and looking all SAS (silent and supportive).

I had a look at him. Mum had been keeping him in the dark, and I wondered if he was a bit on the married side. I hoped he wasn't as I really didn't want Mum to get hurt again. But I also hoped he was, because then she couldn't run off and leave us. What I'm saying is, on the one hand he was a very welcome arrival on our domestic scene; on the other hand he'd better watch his step or I'd have to tear his neck off. He was fifty-ish, like Mum, and not too soft at the edges. But arts, definitely. You still don't get linen jackets on investment bankers. He looked a little scared of me, which was a promising start.

If I was going to go hysterical it would have been now. I imagined myself going into a conversation with Grandmother Beavis, and supplying her lines for her like a ventriloquist.

"Hello Grandmother Beavis. How long have you been like this?"

"Eighty-four years."

"Splendid. And are you based here?"

Mum looked at me again with her caring face. I was in trouble, and that was the thing that concerned her. Once again everything was happening at a very high speed. I said, to no-one in particular: "Did you know Diana was dead?" The PC made a patronising face and I said "No, no, it's on the TV." So Mum picked up the remote and gunned off the sound. She meant to hit the off button but got the mute instead and left it at that.

She said, "Don't be silly, dear," just like she used to when I told porkies as a boy. "Dear" was always significant.

"This is no time for stories," she said. "We don't know anyone called Diana."

"It's not a story," I said. "Well, it is, but it's not."

The W.P.C. had gone over to the body, as we must now call my grandmother, to do her stuff. Mum was making the clicking noises which always mean she's going to cry. Her bloke put an arm round her shoulder and squeezed. I might have minded him doing that, but I didn't. The pictures came and went on the T.V., with only Manny and me knowing the full significance, while in the dark streets all around us the nation had no idea what it would wake up to. Poor old nation.

Now my grandmother was becoming the kid in the corner of the playground who just will not stop being a chimpanzee at the end of break. By holding her wrist, the WPC looked as if she was going to help her up and lead her back to her desk.

"Oh well," said Mum from a wholly different planet, "if she will go around with that Dodi fellow." The boyfriend gave her another squeeze and was clearly very glad he'd come. In the coping stakes he was up there with the WPC and he knew it.

The PC phoned through for an ambulance, and then asked me how I'd got into the flat. Unless it was a trick question, it was a naif thing to ask. If Manny is present there is really no need to ask people how they got there. The PC of all people should have known that. My mother, not knowing who on earth Manny was, looked at him as though he'd got here by mistake. For all I know she thought he'd stepped out of the television, she was looking that loopy. All the same, she sprang to my defence and said: "He used the key. Nicky used the key." I was just going to shake my head at her and say, "No Mum, you had it" when there was a loud noise coming from the heart of the building.

I recognised it at once as the lift motor. It came on and on in a steady drone. A serious intestinal disturbance, amplified for analysis. From the time it was taking, it was clear to me that it was coming up to our floor. But it could hardly be the ambulance men. The PC had barely finished his phone call, and even in the peculiar time system of that night such speed was not possible. We stood and looked at each other, shrugging and inquiring. Me at Mum and her straight back at me. The two Filth at Manny, as if he'd got an associate to come up and join him. My grandmother at everyone and no-one.

The drone cut out like a doodle-bug and the next thing we could hear was the spilling-metal noise of the trellis being shoved aside. It was quite faint. The police must have closed the flat door behind them, unlike Manny and me. The next sounds were of a key in the lock, and agitated voices. There was the Ingersoll scrabbling at the aperture. The door and the hallway were bigging it up it in the silence of the night. There was a struggle with the second lock, and the muffled thud of a shoulder trying to open the door before it was ready. Manny tutted and looked down at his feet. He had a disapproving expression, as if he was having to hear a man deal ineptly with a woman.

After more scrabbling, the door opened and there was a strange voice saying "What the fuck can she keep in here? Crown jewels?"

The PC was hanging cool, being True Hero of Series, savouring the moment when the new arrivals would find they had company. There was a hurried patter of feet in the hall, and the sound of someone running down to the far end of the corridor, followed by a door banging. The PC went out into the hall and crooked a man back into the room with him. It happened as smartly as Kevin's gathering of me into the Leinster from the pavement, except that this bloke was a lot more alarmed than me. At least I knew the pub. This guy was a total stranger in my grandmother's flat.

He looked like he had walked into the middle of a nightmare, which is just about what had happened. A pair of police, three total strangers and an old stiff in the corner. The flat had never seen such a party in its owner's lifetime. This new man must have been about my age, early twenties, which was not a good start for him. A bender had obviously figured somewhere in the programme of the previous twenty-four hours. He had come down from whatever it was, but not totally. Not as far as the knackered and hung-over stage. That joy was waiting. He was in, some would say, the trickiest bit of the cycle, where you're just going to have your cognitive powers refunded but you'd actually rather someone else hung onto them for the moment.

To my total disgust he had mousy dreadlocks grafted onto the bottom of his hair. They'd gone all caked and manky, like the tail of a shitty horse. And he stank. He had another look at my grandmother and was clearly puzzled by her. He took in Manny and the police but dwelt longer on Mum and me. I would say he'd seen something familiar in our faces. A family resemblance maybe. The only thing about him that I recognised, apart from the bingeing stink, was the bunch of keys in his hand: the Ingersolls, the inside-doors crap, and the tricky-bastard Chubb that always hung down lowest from the hook.

The PC, who was in danger of hamming it, said "Just visiting, are we sir?"

The young man bellowed "Alice, Alice!" at the top of his voice, and the PC told him curtly to keep it down if he didn't want to get into even deeper trouble. He didn't actually say trouble, but "doo-doo," which struck me as a bit American for his repertoire. There was a cistern doing its routine, my grandmother's towering old metal thing, the only one of its ilk still living. Alice indeed. This young man's neck I would definitely have to tear off. The WPC was off her marks, but I was ahead of her. Down at the end of the hall a doubled-up girl had rushed out of the karsi and was going into the end room. She looked like she was trying to escape. It was not Alice Alice. Of course it wasn't. I couldn't see her tearing herself away from a nice evening's painting to go shagging with a saddo in an old woman's empty flat. No, it was my sister.

When the WPC and I caught up with her she was hugging herself and hinging at the waist, looking up in terror as if the sky was falling on her. I would say she was off her face by any standards, her eyes lying in mud-pools of mascara and the whole lot tailing down her face into a delta-trickle of black shit diluted by tears. You had to be sharp to glimpse this horror tableau because the curtain of hair came snap over it as her head tossed forward.

"They're getting me," she yelled. "They're getting me." True enough; we were. Someone had to or she'd have knocked her brains out on the corner of some heavy piece. But it wasn't us she was thinking of. She was looking up at the ceiling. There were the great insect shapes of our grandfather's old aeroplane models, moving ever so slightly on their strings as a result of the air disturbance below. "All my life they've been getting me," she cried. "Get them off me. For Christ's sake get them off me."

I have to say the WPC was brilliant. She hugged my sister - properly, not just token - and told her she understood. I don't know if she really did, but she convinced me so much I thought I might ask her for an explanation afterwards. Anyway, she talked her down and held her hand, and the shouting shrank into a whimper. She also put a blanket round her, which had an extraordinary effect, and by the time we were back with the others she looked like a major crash survivor giving her first interview.

My grandmother had vanished. Just for a second it was as if she'd never been and I'd imagined it all and the old woman was still in Devon, healthy as hell. While we had been down in the aeroplane room the ambulance men had come and taken her away, presumably to St. Mary's. So I missed the unprecedented sight of her going without complaint to a state-run facility.

The PC was finishing a long spoken note into his dictaphone. The White Rasta, who turned out to be called Terence, was saying "She's damaged. She's so incredibly damaged." That made Mum bridle and the boyfriend hug her shoulder even harder. I was starting to want to kill people again.

My sister said, "What are the police doing?" She could have meant what are they doing in the flat, or what are they doing on T.V. At this moment the cameras went back to the man in Paris. I could tell from the solemnity of him he was confirming the worst. Manny and I were still the only ones in the room who knew anything at all about the Diana business. I wondered if my sister could even tell the difference between what was in the room before her and what was in the TV. When she looked up and saw Mum, the confusion really bit, and she started crying again. Then she saw me and it got worse. "He'll kill her," she said. She was not sounding hysterical any more, but cold and certain. "He will kill her. He does want her dead."

Oh thanks, Alice. Or sister. Or whatever you want me to call you. You really couldn't have sung more comprehensively than if you were being bankrolled by the prosecution. The WPC took her off into the kitchen for a glass of water and a quiet sit-down, which she should have had a lot earlier in my view. Well done Alice for settling at a stroke every score there ever was between us; for trumping every sleight I have dealt you in the past, and every hurtful action that I could possibly commit towards you in the future. What's for your next trick, Alice? A description to Mum of how Dad really died, complete with corroboration by my Brighton source? I'll see you in the Scrubs, sister, and don't forget to inject the oranges with Smirnoff when you visit.

Manny gave a big laugh, which was meant to show that what Alice had just said was a joke. I thought, well this is the fullest family gathering we've had for a long time; funny how we have to burgle a relative's flat to get together.

It gets a bit blurred again here, not because of me being so knackered but because of the events themselves. To take it carefully: there was more Filth arriving; us all going downstairs; my sister complaining that she was being squashed by the sky, and the W.P.C saying she knew what it felt like; Terence insisting on helping her down the stairs, and his silly dangly legs giving way on the second flight (chivalry's always dodgy, but when you're built like a pipe-cleaner it's a menace);

Mum's boyfriend saying he would do whatever she wanted; people appearing in the streets and saying "She's dead, she's dead," and the P.C. looking on very puzzled and wondering why the old woman should be so important to them; the station officer in the nick being an all right man; Terence talking audibly about Pigs and me telling him to shut the fuck up or I'll stick him; me giving a statement to a DC with Mum there, and the DC intimating they'd need me again; her boyfriend getting the thermos in from the car; my sister being sick for England one more time and going in a cell with a bucket because the toilets were flooding; me asking Mum if we knew any lawyers, and her boyfriend coming up with a few thoughts; the nick being so friendly towards Manny; everyone drinking up the news of the night, deciding on the culprit and declaring it was the end of the line for the Royal Family.

Diana's death was so big that you could feel the heaviness of it come down on the nick. Grown Filth were choking back the tears, even the blokes. You could see their Adam's apples dancing up and down behind their collars. They were thinking of their daughters and nieces, and that was welling out the grief to full belt. One of them said he'd met her once at a hospital up in Haringey. A tiny man brought in for attacking a phone booth shared his grief. I've never been much of a one for the Boys in Blue. It's not actually personal because I think most of them start out as OK individuals and then it all goes wrong when they're in. But I admit to thinking how hard it must be for them sometimes to keep all calm on the outside when they're feeling gutted themselves. Which they obviously were on this Sunday morning when the crowds started going down to the palace with their flowers and teddy bears and God-awful poems.

By dawn one thing was very clear. My grandmother had been, so to speak, buried. For someone so used to upstaging everyone else's troubles, it was a fine come-uppance, and in my view not a moment too soon. As it turned out, she was going to be in very good company in the course of the week. World figures were dropping off the hooks without causing a ripple. Mother Theresa went, and Georg Solti, big trees in anyone's forest. And Jeffrey Bernard, my own personal favourite; one of those bitter, self-obsessed old drunks who gets called a Character because everyone's scared of them; cautionary tale, him. Then there were all the judges, rear-admirals, biochemists and government physicists, all plopping into oblivion with a couple of paragraphs. Even without the Colossus of Dead Diana in the foreground, Grandmother Beavis would have attracted no attention until the publishing of the estates in the local rag. As it was, her profile was nothing. Less than nothing. Virtually an indent.

Back at the house some of the students were still there on the floor, moving a little. I looked carefully to see if there was any sex going on, but there didn't seem to be. It was Mum I was anxious for. I carried my sister upstairs to her bedroom. Terence followed on all fours like an animal backing its way up. I told him he stank like a charnel house, and was pleased to note that he didn't understand. This meant open season for off-beat abuse. At some point we must have lost Manny. I looked round and there was no sign of him. He had spirited himself from the picture.

By now I had stopped trying to work out what everyone did or did not know about Diana and my grandmother. More and more old blokes came on the telly. Mum and me and the boyfriend went into the kitchen and watched it on the black and white without saying a word. Every so often she opened her mouth to have a go, but it didn't come to anything, and died in a sigh. Ditto me. I did manage a big, breathed-out "Sorry" at about 9.30, and she put out her hand and gripped mine hard on the table. The boyfriend, in fairness, was doing well. I think he'd worked out that I wasn't going to take any bonding from him, and he kept good and silent. I was up for tasting the morning in all its drained, no-sleep, monochrome glory. But there was this weight above me, just as heavy as the sky that kept falling on my sister. It was a literal weight of possibilities. Like when I first saw my grandmother slumped against the arm of the settee, there's these different versions and they all seem equally possible. Sometimes, when I'm weirded out from these nights without sleeping, I think the post mortem has proved the old woman's ticker was halted in its tracks by shock when she heard me on the phone tape. Which I suppose would make it manslaughter. Then I think it's Diana who did it by leapfrogging her in the snuffing stakes. Then again I think the pathologist has proved she had it coming anyway, that the coronary was in the pipeline, and I heave a big sigh of reprieve. Round it goes again. Over and over I replay the evening to see if I can find anything else, like a new run of frames in some old footage. But there is nothing there: I enter the flat, hear the voice, clock the telly, see the body. It plays the same, no matter how much I rewind it.

Alice, my girlfriend, isn't coming across as one might have hoped. She says all this goes to show you have to be careful what you pray for in case you get it. I ask her what she means but she only gives me a knowing look and launches off into another top-coat. I try to remember what I may have said to her in the past about my grandmother; whether I banged on to her as well about death being my favoured solution for the old woman. There are times when honesty is a fearful hostage to fortune, specially if you are stoned at the time.

I look at her again, up there on the stepladder, joined to the ceiling by her roller, and I wonder if she is not referring to my grandmother at all, but to Diana. I don't remember saying I wanted Diana out of the way as well, but of course it's perfectly possible. This confusion happens the whole way along. It is a weird merging of what is private and mine and what is public and everybody's. There's the cow-brained lowing for Ma'am to get her royal arse down from Balmoral, and then down she comes looking all tetchy and immovable. "I am your Queen," she says, with those massive powers of observation. I'm yours but not really. She's turned into my grandmother, with that set face, the hard expensive hair, and the look that says nothing's really been up to scratch since the middle of the century. And I keep on thinking, oh, shove over.

The giant dove of flowers goes manky by the palace gates. The fourth day and it's a tip of rotting scent. I think how odd it is that the princess does the dying but all the flowers fetch up on the in-laws' doorstep. I also have a sneaky feeling that Ma'am is chuffed on the quiet. Like Mum with the layers of sorrow and joy in her face when she came into the flat and saw Grandmother Beavis there. The illicit thrill of it. But I can't say any of that. There's still things you're not allowed to say.

There are some crazies in the Leinster who take it further and prove it's really the queen who killed her daughter-in-law (ex). This offends Kevin, who is the fairest republican you could wish for, and wants respect for the dignity of a nation in mourning. The barman says that although Diana was undoubtedly a beautiful woman he never fancied her personally. Blind Landon says "Bagehot" and waits for me to come in with something. Which I do, to the best of my poor ability, but my heart's not in the game. I'm going to stop going to the Leinster.

Everything runs on grief for a week. My public sorrow amounts to nothing and goes undetected in all the howling. My private one is unsayable and goes under lock and key in the cage of me. The First Family turns into a bunch of oppressors and Bambi-killers before your very eyes. They start stinking of poison, like the flowers at their gates. My mother comes and goes with strange composure. But it's as if she's not really here any more. She's got such a peaceful face on, like someone who's got out from under a dirty great debt. All the time she seems about to thank me for something, but it tails into a silent smile. She has some kind of liberty that was not there before, and I want to know how long it will be until I can have mine.

The gun carriage rumbles by. Elton John rolls on his chair like a sad hippo. Great people go glassy in the abbey. Blair's loving it on the quiet. The music's fantastic. It drenches the world in piety and everyone makes another resolution to get into the classics. The black car is brought to a standstill by flowers on the motorway. It vanishes up the drive and everything goes away again. Like the ebbing of a freak tide. All the old landshapes are there, but they take a little getting used to. There's no bail or anything like that, but the Filth want some answers. I know they've seen my sister. They want to see me again. Mum looks at me like she wishes she could help me, but as I say, she's not really there any more. She's shocked, sure. Like everyone else, she's got the Diana business to deal with. But her own Mum's gone, and that's really big. Never mind the Good Innings stuff that comes at her from well-meaning quarters. When something's been around for ever, you miss it all the more when it's gone. Like a local hill vanishing overnight and letting a huge new chunk of sky in. Yes, Mum's absent from us, but she's not in a bad place. She's got the beginnings of freedom in her face. I have the end of it in mine.

The students pad round inaudibly with condolence faces, and offer to make us their top national dishes. I look for Manny in the Leinster but no-one has seen him. I dream he has unorthodox powers of intercession in the law. I dream this dream again and again and again, even in the daytime, standing up, like someone is holding it up in a frame right in front of my nose, no matter which way I turn. My sister has power and punishment in her eyes. The nearness of her freezes me. I assure myself she cannot hurt me as much as she thinks she can. But you must tell me. Please. You're the lawyer.

The End